KATE

KATE

Kathleen Magill

Five Star
Unity, Maine

This novel is a work of fiction. Names, characters, places, and incidents are either the product of the author's imagination, or, if real, used fictitiously.

Five Star First Edition Romance
Published in conjunction with
Kidde, Hoyt & Pickard Literary Agency.

Cover photograph © Alan J. LaVallee.

June 1999
Standard Print Hardcover Edition.

Five Star Standard Print First Edition Romance Series.

The text of this edition is unabridged.

Set in 11 pt. Plantin by Al Chase.

Printed in the United States on permanent paper.

Library of Congress Cataloging in Publication Data

Magill, Kathleen.
    Kate / by Kathleen Magill. — 1st ed.
      p.   cm. — (Five Star first edition romance series)
    ISBN 0-7862-1885-1 (hc : alk. paper)
    I. Title. II. Series.
PS3563.A3474K38 1999
813′.54—dc21
                                        99-13504

To my mother, with eternal gratitude for instilling
her own passion for books in her daughter.
And to GPB, my light across the sea.

I
FAIR PADUA

Katherine had been blessed at birth with all the advantages her society could bestow upon a person, save one.

Born into one of the richest and most powerful families in Padua, she had been given the best education her pleadings and her father's money could buy. As for appearance, from her father she had received her impressive height and from her aristocratic mother she had inherited a certain symmetry of features. Although she could not be called a beauty like her more delicate mother and sister, the strength of her intelligence and character secretly impressed discerning strangers far more favorably than she usually realized.

In short, Katherine had the demeanor, the family, the education and the intelligence that should have insured her success in whatever worldly field of endeavor she might wish to apply herself.

But Katherine had been born a woman.

So all her talents and intellectual accomplishments counted for nothing.

The astrologers consulted prior to her birth in the early years of the eighteenth century predicted — as befitting a first-born — a healthy male child with a glorious future. A child born under the sign of Aquarius, they said, would be clever, versatile, intellectual and strong-willed. But when, on that eagerly awaited day, a healthy female child appeared, the astrologers quickly revised their forecast. The stars now predicted, they said, that the child would be patient, sensitive, placid, and spiritual.

Time was to prove their original prediction the more accurate one.

Fidelia, Katherine's mother, named the babe after Catherine de Medici and then turned her over to servants to raise while she devoted all her time and energies and prayers attempting to produce a male heir. But the only other child to live beyond the first year was another girl, christened Emogena and as unlike Katherine in looks and temperament as two sisters from the same womb could possibly be.

Many of Katherine's earliest memories of her mother revolved around this obsession of Fidelia's to produce a male heir. Katherine remembered how one day, when she was not yet seven, she was summoned to her mother's room after the stillbirth of yet another child. Katherine dreaded entering the blackened room where the shutters were sealed from the fresh air and covered by heavy velvet drapes. The only light came from two candles held by maids. Katherine, frightened by the darkness and the silence and the heavy stench of blood, sweat and incense, was pulled up to the chair where her mother sat.

Fidelia, her face nearly invisible behind a heavy veil, took Katherine's hand and wept. Alarmed, Katherine joined her mother with her own tears although she did not yet understand why her mother grieved so. Other babies had died at birth and her mother had not mourned. But they had been girl babies; this one had been a boy.

Fidelia did not allow the maids to open the shutters for six weeks.

By age four, even the slower-witted Emogena had learned to ask, "Is it a boy?" whenever her mother suddenly disappeared into her room with the women.

But although Fidelia had promised a new altarpiece to the Virgin should she be delivered of a healthy male child, Katherine and Emogena were destined to be the only issue of Ignatius and Fidelia Baptista.

By the time Katherine was eleven, Ignatius, recognizing that he could expect no more issue from Fidelia, publicly declared one Antonio Oliveri to be his sole heir. Antonio, the same age as Katherine, was one of the children of Ignatius and his mistress. By crossing the cardinal's palm, Ignatius legitimized Antonio and brought him to live at the villa.

Unlike Fidelia, Katherine didn't mind Antonio's presence at all. He was someone to play with, to learn fencing with, to ride with — that is, he was until the day he decided that playing with a girl was unseemly. That was the same day that she had laughed when she had beaten him at yet another game of chess.

Katherine remembered that day well for that was also the day that marked the beginning of five years of misery for her — the day Fidelia, wearing black brocade and pearls, summoned Katherine to her room.

"It is time you were learning to be a woman, Katherine. I am told you are fourteen now. Soon you will marry. So you must prepare yourself. You must learn to be a proper wife, a proper woman.

"I am told I have neglected your education, that you are ignorant of the simplest proprieties, that you go off riding at all hours of the day, that you have been known to go off by yourself and read instead of attending to the conversations of your elders.

"This nonsense will stop and it will stop now. I am not pleased with you and neither is your father. He, too, has heard tales of your inappropriate behavior . . ."

"From Antonio I'll wager," Katherine interrupted.

"It does not matter from whom," Fidelia resumed, even

colder than before. "What matters is that you are the daughter of a respected, successful merchant and you have not been acting like one. So I have dismissed all your present tutors . . ."

"What!?"

Fidelia continued as if Katherine had never spoken. ". . . and I have engaged a proper companion for you. Her name is Signorina Lupe. She is a lady of noble birth who, because of a tragic disagreement over her dowry, has never married. I have instructed her to teach you the social arts — the arts you seem to be sorely lacking. She will teach you the womanly graces, the art of pleasing men.

"It is for your own good that you must learn these things.

"The Signorina will be your chaperone, your counselor and, I hope, your confidant. From now on she will accompany you whenever you leave the villa and, to better impart her knowledge, she will share your room with you."

Fidelia, certain she was doing right by her daughter, concluded graciously, "You need never be alone again." Then she smiled and added, "You may kiss me now."

Numb with shock and dismay, Katherine barely remembered touching her lips to her mother's cheek and backing out of the room. But once in the hallway, the cloud on her brain cleared as the full consequences of her mother's actions came to her.

This was intolerable! There must be some way for her to stop this dreadful plan of her mother's. Something she could do or say that would change her mother's mind. But what, she thought frantically. What could a fourteen-year-old do? Appeal to her father? He barely acknowledged her existence, and, from what her mother said, he agreed to this abomination. Appeal to her tutors? They had already been dismissed. Appeal to her aunts and elders? They were the ones whom

Katherine had ignored to satisfy her own adolescent pleasures. They had no particular fondness for such a willful girl. Maybe she could go back to her mother and try to plead with her. But Katherine knew that once her mother was allowed by Ignatius to make a decision on her own, she rarely changed it lest she lose the privilege. Constancy of purpose was, after all, one of the tenets of the righteous path.

The more Katherine thought it over, the more her heart sank. "For your own good" Fidelia had said. For her own good, thought Katherine bitterly, her own mother was engaging a jailer for her, a spy who would watch her, follow her, judge her, report on her every move.

Katherine hated Signorina Lupe before even setting eyes on her.

For what Fidelia did not know or did not care to know or would not understand was that Katherine liked being alone. When Katherine was alone she could dream of doing great deeds, of leaving Padua, of traveling the world, of meeting remarkable persons, of becoming a remarkable person.

But now she would, as her mother said, "never be alone again."

I'll go mad, thought Katherine with a fourteen-year-old's impotent rage. This is the end of the world!

Of course it wasn't the end of the world. Even when Signorina Lupe turned out to be all that Fidelia had promised and all that Katherine had dreaded. Signorina Lupe, although over forty, twittered around as gaily as the eleven-year-old Emogena. She awakened late, then spent hours on her morning toilette, turning Katherine's room into a public thoroughfare. Hairdressers, maids, seamstresses, visitors, all gathered to gossip and primp. Sometimes Signorina Lupe changed dresses five or six times before one met her vain and virtuous approval. Emogena loved the flutter and fuss of these morning hours. Katherine hated it.

Afternoons were no better. Most were spent in music or dancing lessons, usually with several old and idle gentlemen in attendance to exchange the latest witticisms and gossip. Evenings brought even more idle gentlemen, and even more gay chatter.

Katherine's only respite now was early in the morning before her keeper awoke. With no room of her own inside the villa anymore, Katherine simply left it behind. She rode away. Rode away and pretended she was free.

But even then she was not alone. Forbidden to ever leave the grounds without an escort — and stubbornly unwilling to forgive Antonio enough to ask a favor of him — Katherine took to ordering Fidelia's favorite dwarf, Matto, to accompany her. This, Katherine discovered, was almost as good as being alone, for Matto never intruded on her thoughts. He never spoke until he was spoken to and never told her where she could or couldn't go. Most of the time Katherine could even forget he was there behind her.

This one hour of freedom every morning enabled her to endure the rest of the day. It kept her from screaming through the endless round of luncheons, teas, dinners, balls and masquerades during which everyone talked a great deal but no one ever said anything.

Katherine, who had studied Latin and Greek, and who could discuss Newton, Virgil and Horace with any scholastic in Padua, found herself speechless with the strange facile men in wigs who now surrounded her. When once she tried to bring up a recently published book with a visitor from Venice who seemed more intellectually advanced than the usual visitor, he only smiled in reply and quoted Erasmus to her: "Books destroy women's brains, who have little enough of themselves."

Thereafter Katherine usually kept her mouth shut and let the willing Emogena carry the conversations. Emogena had idolized Signorina Lupe and learned well from her.

It was consequently that over the next few years Emogena gradually became known throughout Padua as "La Bella Emogena." Katherine was known as "The Other One," or "The Older One."

Attracted by Emogena's pert vivacity, suitors lined up for her favors with a zealous ardor. Attracted by Katherine's father's gold, suitors lined up for Katherine's favors with a grim resolution.

Katherine knew what was going on. After all, she had read Rabelais at thirteen.

Night after night after the visitors had finally left and she crawled into bed, Katherine devised strategies of escape — fantastic strategies, murderous strategies, miraculous strategies — all too extreme, all too impractical.

And then one night as she listened to Signorina Lupe's heavy breathing beside her, the solution came to her in a flash. If she wanted to be left alone, she need only act in such an unpleasant way that others would be happy to leave her alone. She would listen to Signorina Lupe's counsel, and then act in the exact opposite way. She would become forward, contentious, peevish, and rebellious.

She would become a shrew.

The next day she set her plan in motion. Instead of witty remarks, she made sarcastic ones; instead of hiding her classical education, she flaunted it by correcting any pompous male who erred; instead of flattering her suitors, she disparaged them. And beat them at chess.

The scheme worked in the beginning. Soon Katherine had plenty of time to herself, to study, to ride, to read, to dream again. Her temper even drove Signorina Lupe out of her room at last and into Emogena's. This delighted Emogena for not only did Emogena enjoy Signorina Lupe's attention, but she was also afraid of the dark and hated to be alone.

But the day Signorina Lupe changed rooms was the day she chose to reveal another side of herself to Katherine. Because for all her frivolity, the Signorina was not the stupid fool that the smug young Katherine had judged her to be. As she supervised the removal of her finery from Katherine's room, Signorina Lupe caught the triumphant look in Katherine's eyes and pulled her aside.

"Do not think that I do not know what you are doing, my haughty young girl. Or that others will not figure it out." Katherine's expression changed as the Signorina continued. "Do you think you are the only woman with a brain, the only woman to try to rise up against her fate?

"There have been thousands like you, there will be thousands more. You think you have won something now because all the suitors are gone. Because none considered your dowry a sufficient compensation for living with your temper.

"But I'll tell you something. The truth. You have won nothing. Nothing! Only a little time, that's all. You will never win. You cannot win. You are a woman and a woman's place is in a man's bed. Or Christ's bed. Or she does not exist. Like I do not exist.

"Do you want my life, Katherine? Eh? No room of my own, no home of my own, no money of my own, no husband, no children, no family of my own?

"Keep rejecting the suitors, Katherine, and your life will wind up a hell like mine."

Her words sobered Katherine. It had never occurred to her that Signorina Lupe might have found her chain to Katherine as objectionable as Katherine herself did. With all the

14

blindness and self-centeredness of youth, it had never occurred to Katherine that anyone else could have any feelings as deep as her own.

But when the older woman and all her things were gone from her room, Katherine instantly forgot the Signorina's warning and her euphoria returned.

Free at last! That was all that Katherine could see that mattered. She was a fully grown young woman of almost twenty, with no inclination toward marriage or toward the church. Her parents would now have to give up their attempts to marry her off. She dismissed Signorina Lupe's warning. The Signorina was just upset and wanted to make Katherine feel bad. Her words meant nothing now that Katherine was alone to do as she pleased.

Or so she thought.

II

TO WIVE

After mass and chocolate on a November morning of her twentieth year Katherine was summoned to the library. There her mother sat, stiff and silent; there her father stood, tall and stern. Deferring to him, Katherine curtseyed.

Her father came directly to the point. "I have come to an agreement with one Cesaro Benno of Verona for your hand," he said impassively. "He is willing to marry you in exchange for the sum of six thousand ducats. A heavy price, true, but he has heard of your reputation and will accept no less."

Katherine, shocked, grabbed hold of the back of a chair to steady herself. Aware of her heart pounding against her tight corset, she tried to object. "I am not going to marry someone I have never met!"

Her father paid no attention to her outburst, just continued his speech as if Katherine had never opened her mouth. "The ceremony will be held Christmas week. I know that is short notice for your mother, but Emogena's wedding is contracted for April and you must be married before your younger sister."

"But why?" protested Katherine.

"Because that is the way things are done."

Katherine tried again. "But everything has been so perfect recently. Why should it change? Why should you want me to marry?"

"I assume, Katherine, that when you say that everything has been so perfect recently you mean that everything has been so perfect for *you*. You have never considered that it might not be so perfect for anyone else. You have had your way for too long now." Ignatius raised his hand to stop her from speaking. "Don't bother arguing with me, it won't do any good. I do not wish to hear your opinion on the matter for you are not entitled to have an opinion on the matter.

"If you refuse to go through with this marriage," he continued, "I will put you into a convent. Would you prefer that? It does not matter to me. Actually, the nunnery would be less expensive than a husband."

He read her face. "No, I did not think so. But it is your choice. Your only choice. You have been nothing but trouble to me recently and I mean to be rid of you one way or another. Your mother claims you've fallen under a witch's spell, that you're possessed. I myself do not believe in witches, but I do believe you are possessed. You're possessed of a rebellious character, you're possessed of a shameless pride, you're possessed of a headstrong — and unseemly — passion for unwomanly subjects.

"Nevertheless, I do give you a choice. Signore Benno or the cloister. Should you wish to meet Signore Benno before you make your choice you will have that opportunity. He will be in Padua next week to sign the papers and to look you over. I will present you to him and I expect you to keep a civil tongue in your head.

"That is all."

He turned his back on his wife and daughter to indicate the interview was at an end. Fidelia obligingly rose, curtseyed to his stiff back, and pulled Katherine toward the door. As she unlatched the library door, the sounds of scampering footsteps receded down the hall.

You have been nothing but trouble to me . . . I mean to be rid of you . . . . The words echoed in Katherine's stunned brain.

How could her father say those things? It was almost as if he hated her, as if the very sight of her offended him. But how could that be so? Ignatius used to be so proud of her when she was a child, proud of her intelligence, her quick wit, her resemblance to him. He used to dress her as a boy and take her to fencing and riding lessons. Until Antonio arrived, she was the only one of the family allowed to look through his precious telescope. And when she expressed enough interest in what she saw there, he was the one who took her to Pere d'Amboise. He was the one who instructed the Jesuit to teach her Galileo, Kepler and Newton.

But, as Katherine remembered, it was when she learned them that her father's attitude toward her had changed. Pere d'Amboise, delighted with his young charge's eagerness and aptitude, taught her the mysteries of science. Katherine enjoyed the attention, enjoyed the challenge to her mind, and the more difficult the subject, the more she enjoyed it. It was thus she developed her intellectual keenness, her critical faculty, her power of concentration. But in so doing, it was thus she also developed her will and her pride.

Others less gifted than she became her victims. Complaints reached the ears of her father. A young girl was not supposed to be so bold with her tongue as Katherine, so audacious, so impudent. And so her father, who paid close attention to what others thought, came to believe that educating her as if she were a boy had been a grievous mistake. He came to regret it. But Katherine never did. Katherine saw in her education a refuge, a compensation for restrictions of being born the wrong sex.

Now, to escape both this marriage arrangement and the nunnery, she would need more than her well-trained intellect, she would need some canny chicanery. From Machiavelli and Signorina Lupe she had learned manipulation, but manipulation required time, and time was the one thing she did not have.

After shaking free of her mother and calming down somewhat, Katherine passed Emogena in the hallway. She thought she read a smirk on her sister's vapid face. The news of the impending marriage had apparently already spread.

Stopping Emogena, Katherine demanded, "Have you seen Matto?"

"No, sister," smiled Emogena. "No need for *more* entertainment today."

To Emogena, Matto was less than a servant. He was a pet dog, able to turn somersaults, juggle, dance or sing whenever she was bored. She commanded, he obeyed — adroitly, artfully, and merrily.

Until six years before, Katherine had not treated the little man much better than her sister did now. In truth, she had barely been aware of him. But all that changed along with everything else when she was fourteen. On that long-ago day when she wished to go riding, no relative or bastard brother had been available to accompany her. Annoyed and frustrated, the girl spotted the jester by the stable door. "Can you ride?" she demanded. "Yes, Mistress." he replied with a bow. "Get him a horse," she ordered the stable attendant. The horrified attendant protested, "You cannot go out with him. He is not a proper chaperone for a young lady. Your mother will blame me!"

But Katherine ignored his protests and once again ordered a horse brought for the dwarf along with Cybele, her favorite mount. The attendant capitulated and brought her what she wanted. There was a further delay while the stirrups were adjusted for Matto. But once atop a horse, Matto looked almost normal. Katherine even smiled at him, although pleased more with the scandal she was causing than with the man himself. "You shall be my official escort from now on," she decreed as she spurred Cybele.

When out of sight of the villa, Katherine rode fast and furious. At first Matto found it hard to keep up with her. But he always did. She had given him no other choice. When they rode together after that first day he carefully managed to stay behind her, silent unless spoken to first, the coral pendant around his neck bouncing in the air with every jog of the horse. And when it was time to turn back, for there was nowhere to go but back, Katherine would slow down and sometimes talk to him.

One day she asked him what the coral pendant was for. "The evil eye, Mistress. Malocchio. Coral protects one against the malocchio."

This sounded almost blasphemous to the fourteen-year-old. "Do you not believe God protects you?"

"Of course, Mistress. But I am so short, perhaps God cannot see me all the time. So I wear the coral just in case."

Katherine considered the logic of his words, and concluded it had merit. Or that it at least was harmless. And thus their relationship started.

For six years they rode together. He eventually could read her moods, although she could never read his. Matto taught Katherine ballads that she would have never learned in her father's drawing room, or in the books of her father's library. Books had taught her the wisdom of the mighty, Matto taught her the wisdom of the fallen.

Consequently, the day Katherine's father announced her future to her, she sought out the dwarf. She found him in the bustling kitchen. As she entered, all conversation stopped instantly. "Come," she ordered Matto, ignoring the stares of the others. No doubt he had heard of the meeting with her father. All the servants had probably heard of it. But Matto was smart enough to give no indication of anything amiss.

Katherine did not speak again until they were astride their mounts. And then she only said, "No jokes, no prattle today." And Matto nodded and off they rode.

For the next two hours Katherine brooded over her situation. Did she truly only have two choices as her father claimed? Marriage or the nunnery? Katherine could not accept that that was all her life could be, would be. Antonio, Katherine thought bitterly, was off traveling through France with a tutor. With each passing year, the world at Antonio's fingertips had opened and expanded. It seemed as if hers had contracted and shrunk.

But surely there had to be some alternative. Some third or even fourth choice. But she just couldn't think of one.

Matto finally broke the silence. "Are you all right, Mistress?" he asked.

"Do I not act all right?"

"As a matter of fact, you don't."

Katherine turned to the little man and decided to trust him with her thoughts. "Some say that I am bewitched and that demons have taken control of me."

"Some say," he replied in kind as if she had merely started one of their word games, "that deformed fellows like me were sired by demons."

"Some say I might even be a witch myself."

"Some say I might even be a demon myself."

"Are you a demon, Matto?"

"Do you believe in demons?"

"No."

"Then I am not a demon. Are you a witch?"

"Do you believe in witches?"

"Yes," he answered, to Katherine's surprise. "But I don't believe you're one."

I wish I were, thought Katherine. *Then I might find a way out of this mess.*

The silence between them grew as Katherine turned her attention inward once again. *Why was her father so against her? And why did her mother always take his side?* Katherine sometimes suspected that her mother hated her father. But she knew that Fidelia would support his wishes to her dying day. So she could not turn to her mother. Nor to any relative in fact. They would all side with her father. It seemed there was no one Katherine could turn to.

Or was there?

Yes, thought Katherine, *there is one person. One who could surely help her find a way out. One man who used to have an answer to all my questions. One man who truly loved me because he loved my spirit, my soul. Didn't he tell me so once?*

Pere d'Amboise would have an answer. He could save her. He had opened worlds for her. He could not stand by and let those worlds be shut to her. He could not.

So, with Matto following behind her, a hopeful Katherine spurred Cybele toward the basilica.

III

UNDER THE NAME OF PERFECT LOVE

Pere d'Amboise was a tall, elegant man, not yet forty, who had taught science and mathematics at the University for twelve years. Originally from Lyons, he had been educated at universities in Rome and Madrid. When Ignatius had officially stopped his daughter's formal education, she herself arranged to study with Pere d'Amboise clandestinely when her family thought that she was devoutly attending special mass. The deception did not bother her for she saw no other way to stay in touch with the great ideas of the world. Women were not allowed in the coffeehouse next to the apothecary shop where all the local men of letters met. Pere d'Amboise was her sole link to that exciting and forbidden world.

It was he who had taught her a love of languages, of poetry, of mathematics, of architecture. Consequently, to Katherine when she was very young, his knowledge seemed infinite. And although she was no longer so very young, and she no longer believed his knowledge limitless, she still believed he could help her find a way out. Her father not only respected the man, he listened to him. So all she had to do was ask her revered old teacher to champion her cause. He could not refuse.

For he had failed her once; he would not dare to fail her again.

When Katherine was thirteen she, briefly and almost inevitably, had fallen in love with the priest. She had even expressed her love to him. Katherine remembered the occasion well. He had been at his narrow desk and she had been sitting opposite him. They had been translating Lucretius. Katherine playfully taunted him with the words there before them, with the words that equated religion with superstition and fear of death.

To her surprise, he agreed. "Yes," he said, "many of our beliefs are based on superstition."

Uneasy at such frankness in such a holy place, Katherine checked around her before responding, "Are you not afraid of someone overhearing you?"

"I am a man of reason and I believe men of reason must have a reasonable religion," he said. "But I do not believe reason and faith are contradictory. Reason is the way to faith. I use my reason to purify the faith." Here his voice rose, reflecting the passion of his belief. "We must purify the faith of these power-hungry, quarrelsome church fathers."

For the first time Katherine felt a genuine fear for him. Although flattered that he had confided in her, even at thirteen she knew how dangerous it was to speak one's mind against the absolute authority of the Church. "Please be more cautious, father," she had urged.

He smiled at her concern and took her hand. As he did so she felt the heat from his touch rise up her arm. She flushed.

"Dear child, do you fear for me?" She nodded, aware of little but his hand on hers.

"That is very sweet of you. But there is no need for you to fear. I have the true faith. Have you none?"

Katherine breathed deeply. Her extreme youth when combined with his hand on hers gave her reckless courage. "I have faith in you," she blurted.

The instant she said the words she regretted them. For he immediately withdrew his hand and pulled his spine up and back. And she watched the man retreat behind the priest.

"Katherine," he began in such a cold impersonal tone that both her hopes and heart sank, "I am your teacher. And you are my pupil. That is our relationship. That is our only relationship. That can be our only relationship."

Katherine, in despair, took another childish chance. "I love you," she confessed.

She saw the fear flash across his dark eyes. But he did not say anything for quite a while. As the silence grew heavier, Katherine realized she had made a tactical error by speaking of her love. Desperate from discomfort and dashed hopes, she broke the silence. "Am I truly just a pupil to you? A pupil not unlike a hundred others you have had? Do you not feel something different for me, something more?"

For the first time since she had known the priest and scholar, he avoided her eyes. And Katherine remembered how he seldom looked at women directly in the eyes. But until that moment he had always looked in hers. Did that mean he had never thought of her as a woman until now?

He finally raised his eyes from the weighty Latin tome sitting on the desk between them and spoke. "Katherine, I do not deny that I have often felt a special affinity for you," he began. "Sometimes it is as if our two minds, our two souls, are one."

Katherine's hopes rose but still he did not meet her eyes. "I have accepted this as God's gracious gift to us, as indeed almost the greatest gift He can give two persons. I suppose it could be called a love, but a love of the spirit only, not of the material, not of the flesh."

He finally met her eyes as he repeated, "Never of the flesh." This time it was Katherine who looked away. The priest continued. "The sin of the flesh is the greatest of all sins. Our love, however, is untainted by this sin and shall remain untainted. And we should be properly grateful for it."

But Katherine's thirteen-year-old heart didn't want a love of the spirit. Her heart wanted a love of flesh and blood, for she was made of flesh and blood. She at least wanted to feel his hand on hers again. She liked that feeling and wanted it to continue.

Did his heart not beat fast like hers when they touched? Did he not feel the temperature of his body change, the color of his skin change? And were these not signs of the flesh? How could he deny them?

But deny them he did. And, with sinking hope, Katherine recognized that he always would deny them. The spiritual held more charm for him than the material. True, he said he could see their two souls as one. But he had said nothing of their two bodies ever being as one. And he never would.

And so did Katherine finally accept that she couldn't always get what she wanted. Her first disappointment in love marked the last day of her childhood. She and the priest still met over the years and he still recommended various books for her to study. But never again did they speak of personal matters, of matters which caused the blood to rise up.

Seven years had passed since that day. And now it was another grey morning. And now it was time to speak once again of personal matters, of flesh and blood matters. As Katherine strode through the familiar labyrinth of corridors, she was vaguely aware of the stares of disapproval she garnered for her muddy riding habit. Such behavior would certainly be reported to her family, and her inappropriate dress used as more fuel for the fire of her father's displeasure with her. Oh well, she would apologize later. More important things had to be taken care of first.

Katherine found Pere d'Amboise at his telescope in a state

of excitement. When his attendant announced her, the priest quickly called her over to the window.

"Come look through my new treasure, Katherine. You can see the spots on the sun."

Katherine, although hardly in a mood for a science lesson that morning, respectfully obeyed him and looked.

"Do you see?" he asked impatiently. Katherine nodded and walked away. He immediately took her place at the glass and continued speaking, oblivious to her in his own exhilaration. "I had read of them but this is the first I have seen of them myself. Now that I have seen them for myself I know their existence to be true. I know them to be a fact. Isn't that what I have always taught you? See for yourself. Observe the thing itself. Be directed by facts."

Katherine could keep silent no longer. "I have a fact for you."

"Yes, Katherine?" he asked, still looking through the telescope.

"The fact is I am about to be married off."

That finally diverted his attention from the glass. He turned, noticed her untidy appearance, her agitation. Without another word he capped his precious glass and gestured for her to be seated. "Now what did you wish to see me about?"

"My father informed me this morning that he had arranged a marriage for me. And it seems I am to have absolutely no say in the matter!" She stopped, looked up at him and waited for him to comfort her, to tell her it must be a mistake, he would look into it and make everything right again.

But Pere d'Amboise did not speak. Instead, he got up and walked around his great carved desk and sat behind it, as if wishing to put a greater distance between them. Then, steepling his smooth soft hands in front of his face he finally spoke. But he spoke words she did not wish to hear, words she had not come to hear.

"Katherine, you have been of age for some years now. Indeed, some would say you are overaged. So surely such news from your father could not be totally unexpected."

"Of course it was unexpected." His calmness aggravated her. "He never consulted me, he never asked me what I wished for my future. He has given me no say in my future!"

"As I understand it, Katherine, you do have a say. As I understand it, your father has allowed you the option of entering the service of God."

Katherine finally caught on. *So,* she thought, *he knows all about it. And if he knows about it then all of Padua must know about it. But he could still help, couldn't he?*

"Yes," she acknowledged, "he gave me that option. But surely you know me by now. I have no desire to be a saint. Like you do."

His eyes told her he knew what she meant. The priest looked away first.

"I am not a saint."

"You act like one." Katherine immediately regretted the caustic words and bit her tongue. She could not risk his turning away. She needed his help too much now.

"Don't worry," she hastened to add, "I am not here to set traps for your chastity. I have come to ask you to help me, to do something, or to tell me what to do. Have you withdrawn so far from life," she pleaded, rising to her feet, "that you have no compassion for those of us who still walk on the earth?"

"Katherine, be fair!"

"I am sorry, father, if I have offended you." But she was not sorry.

"If you will be seated we will discuss this like the two reasonable beings we both are. I assume you are still a reasonable being?"

Katherine nodded. "Of course I am. But my father, my family, they find my viewpoint preposterous, my desires ridiculous."

"Have you considered their viewpoint, their desires?"

"That's all I ever hear. Their viewpoint."

"But do you understand it? Think a moment now. Here we have your father, a man with two daughters, a prosperous man whose fortune depends greatly upon his status in the community. He is, in general, a good man, a man who believes in following the rules and traditions that were established centuries before his time."

Katherine looked at the priest as if to ask "So?"

"And one of those valuable traditions is to obtain the best possible matches for one's children. Is not such a thing only natural, only reasonable? Does not God's Holy Word, the Bible, demand that he do such a thing for his children?

"Why then should you object when he is only trying to do what is right by you?"

"But how does he know what is right by me? He's never asked me," Katherine objected.

"He knows it is right because it is what God demands."

"God demands that I marry a stranger from Verona?"

"God demands that a daughter do her duty and obey her father."

"But what if the father is wrong? What if the tradition is wrong?"

"I sometimes regret teaching you the art of polemics, Katherine! You do exasperate me. Do you believe, like Luther, that all the great minds before you knew nothing, that you alone know what's right, what's good? That you know God's will?"

"I know what you taught me."

"Do not play with me, Katherine. I do not find heresy amusing."

"You taught me that I have eyes to see with, that I have a mind to think with. To examine. To judge for myself. Is that also what Luther believed?"

"Luther was a heretic!" Pere d'Amboise's tone suddenly chilled her. "Obviously I have failed as a teacher if I have not taught you that there is something greater than facts, and something greater than you. I assumed that you, with your clever mind that you're so proud of, knew that. I am a man of God as well as a scientist. As a man of God I have learned duty, obedience, acceptance. It seems you must learn it also."

Katherine considered his words, analyzed them, and then asked, "Suppose the Church told you there are no spots on the sun? Suppose the Church told you something you knew not to be true? Would you not reject their judgment on the basis of the evidence before you?"

"No, I would not."

"Father!" Katherine could not believe this sudden turnabout. She looked at him as if he had betrayed her.

The priest closed his eyes. When he opened them again he looked older to her. "How do I know the truth, Katherine? How can any mortal man? Or woman? If the Church, which I accept as infinitely greater than myself, tells me that what seems to me to be white is black, then I must believe it."

"Well I do not! The Church is made of men, fallible men. Why should fallible men be able to change facts? What's white is white and what's black is black."

"Beware Katherine. Though my love and patience for you is great, you are beginning to sound like a heretic."

Katherine walked over to the window and considered carefully before she spoke again. "You just said you loved me.

Were I a heretic, would you still love me?"

"Yes. I would still love a heretic. But listen to me now. Although my love is great, I would do as Paul IV said. 'Even if my own father were a heretic, I would gather wood to burn him.' "

Katherine turned, looked in his eyes, and saw he meant what he said. He would burn her. And any other disobedient disbeliever.

"What a fool I was to come here. I had hoped to find a man. Instead I found nothing but a priest. And priests do love sacrifices, don't they? Their own sacrifices as well as everyone else's.

"Well, I'm not going to be your sacrifice or your Church's sacrifice or my father's sacrifice. Please excuse me for bothering you."

She turned to leave but before she reached the door he cut her off. Grabbing her arm, he entreated, "Katherine!"

"Yes?" she replied indifferently and in control of her emotions at last. He recognized his defeat and released her arm.

"Nothing." He paused and closed with his usual parting phrase. "God be with you, Katherine."

"And with you, father," she replied.

As the door closed between them she dipped into a perfunctory curtsey.

On the way home with Matto, she restrained Cybele to a walk. There was no hurry now.

But now Matto wanted to talk.

"Did you get your miracle, Mistress?" he asked as he trotted up beside her.

"I do not believe in miracles."

"So the priest did not help you then?"

"The priest is a man of God. And men of God believe in doing one's duty whatever the price."

Katherine was suddenly weary of the subject and could no longer hide her despair. "No, Matto, the priest could not help me. It seems I will marry Signore Benno."

"Perhaps this Signore Benno is not a bad man."

"Perhaps."

"Then all your present worries will be for nothing."

When she did not reply, he continued, "Perhaps this Signore Benno will be a veritable prince of a man."

She looked at the man beside her to see if he were mocking her. But so what if he was? She joined in his game, weakly at first.

"Perhaps he will be a paragon of virtue."

"And an Adonis," responded Matto.

"An Apollo," countered Katherine.

"A hero."

"A demi-god."

"An angel."

"Wait," cried Katherine, "no more angels. Please! I've had enough of the pure in heart and soul and mind. What I need is an earthly rogue. That is my only hope now. That this man they would have me spend the rest of my life with is the man whom, had I been given the choice, I would have chosen. If not . . . I am lost. There is no one left who can help me."

"Oh, you are wrong, Mistress."

Matto so seldom contradicted her that she pulled up Cybele to stare at him.

"There is one left who can help you." He seemed to be teasing her but he wasn't smiling.

"Who?" she demanded. "Do you mean God, Matto? I thought you were not a religious man."

"Oh, not God, Mistress Katherine. One much lower. Much, much lower. In fact, the lowest of God's creatures."

"Stop speaking in riddles. Whom do you mean? Who is the

lowest of creatures who can help me? Right now I feel myself to be the lowest. Are you telling me to help myself?"

"No, I am telling you that if you but open your eyes, you'll find the solution in front of you. But I think you are not yet desperate enough to see the one who might save you. And of course it would require a heavy payment on your part. A very heavy payment. But then all things worthwhile have a price, no? So what is it worth to you to get out of this marriage? What price are you willing to pay? How far are you willing to go?"

Then the dwarf shut up and refused to speak further. So Katherine, annoyed with his enigmatic innuendos, spurred Cybele forward and left Matto to follow as best he could.

IV
LORDS AND HUSBANDS

Katherine, Emogena, Fidelia, and Signorina Lupe sat stiffly in their brocade gowns in the hallway that linked the library with the great reception hall and awaited Ignatius and the two prospective sons-in-law.

With the wedding just two weeks off, hundreds of details still had to be worked out. Already the villa buzzed with guests — relatives Katherine had never seen, business associates of her father, lesser political figures who must not be offended by being excluded from the wedding of the daughter of one of Padua's leading citizens. Even the Venetian court had sent a representative.

Extra cooks, servants and grooms had all been hired. Crises occurred almost hourly, crises which could only be handled by Fidelia. Ignatius, as usual, had left all the domestic details to his wife. Fidelia, as usual, had managed.

Never had Fidelia been so busy. For two weeks she had not been able to rest in one place without an interruption. But now she sat, uninterrupted, for an hour ago Cesaro Benno had arrived with Philemon, Emogena's intended. They had immediately secluded themselves with Ignatius in the library. The women were obliged to wait for them outside the library's doors.

Emogena, of course, had already met Philemon. Of all the suitors for her hand, he was the one who had pleased her the most, the one whom she had begged her father to accept. It was Philemon who had subsequently found Cesaro . . . for

Philemon realized he had no hope of a speedy marriage to the pretty Emogena unless the elder sister had been disposed of in some way.

And so the four women sat, too nervous to read or sew, too tense to talk. In the silence Katherine imagined she could hear her own heart beating. She had already broken out into a light sweat. Finally, she could sit no longer. Up she rose, only to pace the hallway back and forth. Every time she reached the window at the end of the hallway she could see the newly hired workers scrubbing the fountains and statues in the garden.

"Katherine," her mother finally ordered, "sit!"

Katherine sat.

With nothing else to do, she ran her eyes over the items in the familiar hallway. In the twenty-one years of her marriage, Fidelia had channeled most of her energy into collecting art. The result was that paintings, sculptures, plates, tiles, books, jewels and miscellaneous curios choked every space of the villa's rooms and hallways. Her mother pursued art as Pere d'Amboise pursued God, as her father pursued position, as Katherine herself pursued freedom. But, looking around now at the evidence of Fidelia's passion, it seemed to Katherine that it might be more accurate to say not that her mother possessed art, but that art possessed her mother.

Many of the paintings her mother had chosen over the years made her smile. Pere d'Amboise, as her teacher, had allowed Katherine to study every subject but one. He refused to let her look at any medical texts, deeming the human body not a proper subject. Little did he realize that pictures of naked bodies stared down at Katherine from every wall of the villa. Interspersed with the requisite dark paintings of Madonnas and martyrs were great lush nudes by Tintoretto, Titian and Rubens. *Venus and Adonis. Venus and Amor.*

Anatomy was no mystery in Katherine's household.

The click of the door latch startled the four women from their private thoughts. They immediately rose and prepared themselves as three men emerged from the library — Ignatius first, then Emogena's suitor Philemon, and finally Cesaro Benno.

As her father introduced the two younger men Katherine heard not one word for she was dumbfounded at the sight of Cesaro.

Not only was the man standing before her nowhere near the Adonis that she and Matto had joked about, but he was at least twice her age, twice her weight, and a good half foot shorter. The broken veins in his face told her he was a heavy drinker, his darting eyes told her he was a reprobate, and his elaborately curled wig told her he was a popinjay. Even Fidelia seemed momentarily taken aback at his appearance, but she quickly recovered. With her usual icy graciousness, she welcomed the visitors.

Katherine herself could barely curtsey to Cesaro as the two were introduced. Her sweat turned cold as she felt him run his small black eyes over her, appraising her as her father would appraise a falcon or her mother a gold medallion. She felt she could almost hear him thinking, *Have I made a good bargain?*

"Good morrow, Kate," he said. When she did not reply he continued the opening pleasantries. "So you are the Katherine who is to be my wife. I am told that you are rough and waspish and wild. And that you have quite a tongue in you. But you seem passing courteous to me."

"Katherine," quizzed her father, "have you nothing to say?" She shook her head, too overwhelmed to open her mouth. "Well, my dear, I must say that's a pleasant surprise. I will assume, then, you have no objections?"

The question offered Katherine her chance, if only she could gather her wits together. But before she could reply, Cesaro spoke first. "What good would any objections be?" He looked up at Katherine and tightly smiled, "Your noble father and I have agreed that you shall be my wife. The matter of your dowry has been settled. The contracts have just now been signed. And the Sunday after next will be our wedding day."

More unbearable news! *Never!* she wanted to scream, but the cry strangled in her throat.

Ignatius took charge once again. "So things are settled at last. Good. Now let us celebrate over the finest table in Padua." With a wave of Ignatius's hand, a servant flung open the double and triple doors to the great reception room where dozens of eager guests waited to descend upon the two betrothed couples.

The feast began. Later Katherine wondered how she got through that long afternoon, that afternoon in which her misfortune was toasted from every corner. Food, drink and laughter surrounded her although she herself neither ate, nor drank, nor laughed. Instead, she stood tall and still in the furthest corner of the great hall, forbidden to leave. How she wished then that her mother had followed the court fad of masks; if so, she would not then feel so exposed under the constant stares. The only one present who did not curiously glance her way was Cesaro. He alone appeared oblivious to her, although far from oblivious to the wine and food.

Strangely, it was Signorina Lupe, her antagonist for so many years, who came to Katherine's aid. She stood by her the whole time, fending off the well-wishers, directing the conversation away from Katherine, making sweet lying excuses for her, and wiping her brow when the sweat became too visible. With all the outside doors shut tightly against the cold winter air, and all the fires lit, and all the bodies pressed against each other, Katherine felt her own body burning up.

Finally, after what seemed to be the longest five hours of her life, Fidelia signaled to Katherine that she could leave. Signorina Lupe left with her, accompanied her up the great marble staircase to her room, eased her down on the bed, removed her shoes, and even closed the drapes for her. Then, without a single word, the older woman left Katherine alone upstairs in the darkness. Downstairs, the candles were lit and the party continued.

It took more than an hour for Katherine's benumbed muscles to unclench. When they finally relaxed, the exhausted Katherine slept.

When she awakened it was well past midnight. She had slept for over six hours. The healing sleep had cleared her head and her will. And with her mind's return, her senses returned. The sense that came back the sharpest was one of hunger. She had eaten nothing since the morning; now her stomach demanded food.

Knowing no one would be about at such a late hour, she didn't bother redoing her toilette. With her hair falling down and in rumpled clothes and stockinged feet, Katherine scampered down to the kitchen. There, just as she had expected, lay the remnants of that evening's banquet. She uncorked a bottle of wine and settled down to her own private feast.

When she could eat no more she propped her feet up on the table and retraced the day's events. Comforted now by the sleep and the food, she thought perhaps she had overreacted. True, Cesaro was nothing to look at, but she was no beauty herself. True, he was older than she but were not most men older than their wives? Yes, concluded Katherine charitably, it was wrong to judge by appearances alone. She would do the balanced, rational thing and give the man from Verona another chance.

Having made up her mind, Katherine left the scraps of her meal for the dogs and emptied the remainder of the bottle of wine into her glass. Then, glass in one hand and candle in the other, she headed for the back entrance of the library. She would seek solace and comfort in a book, perhaps a book of the love thoughts of Ovid to get her in a mood for marriage.

But when she entered the antechamber she at once heard voices coming from the library. Quickly she blew out her candle and crept closer to the doorway to investigate. She kept her presence hidden for it would not be proper for guests to see the daughter of the house in such a disheveled state.

Just outside the doorway she could hear the voices clearly but she could not see to whom they belonged without exposing herself. The voices were those of two very drunken men. The voices were those of Philemon and Cesaro.

"I tell you I would not wed her for a mine of gold," said the first voice.

"That tells me you do not yet know the effect of gold," said the other.

"How much did he offer you anyway?"

"Six thousand ducats upon the marriage. After his death, one-eighth of all his lands."

"Ah, Cesaro, I salute you! I envy you! He did not offer me such bounty for Emogena."

" 'Woo her, wed her, bed her, and rid the house of her,' that's what the old man told me. And that's what I agreed to do. So everything works out splendidly, no small thanks to you for putting me on to her. The father gets rid of her and I get the money-lenders off my back."

"And you get Katherine, the greatest shrew in the Venetian Republic."

"As I have told you many times, I want a wealthy wife, that is my one and only requirement. I care nothing for her age, her looks, her temperament, or whether she loves me or not. She can be the greatest shrew in the whole of Italy, in the whole of Christendom, it would not matter in the least. Give me enough ducats and I will wed a hound from hell! So my young friend, here's a salute to you again for finding her."

At the clinking of the glasses Katherine sank to the floor. She hugged her knees against her chest and concentrated on the activity in the next room. She did not have to wait long to learn more.

"Still, she's not a bad-looking woman, if you like the stately type. Emogena tells me she's actually quite accomplished, quite the little scholar. And religious, too. Used to see a priest almost every day."

"Oh," Cesaro interrupted, "so now that she's out of the way, now that you're free to marry the fair sister, the cursed Katherine is not so bad, hey? Well, if you truly feel that way, would you care to trade sisters?"

"Never!" laughed Philemon. "I don't have your greed."

"You don't have my need. Or my guts, my young friend! Don't try and tell me what sort of woman my intended is. Remember I've been married before. And I've probably slept with 500 women in my time. That Katherine upstairs is every bit the cursed bitch we've heard she is. She didn't fool me with her silence today. She's a willful, shrewd vixen. But that's because she has had no master. Until now. Give me two weeks after the ceremony and I'll be the master of her. I will own her like I own my house, my horse, and my dogs. And she will know it and act accordingly."

"I hardly think the Katherine I've heard of will agree to that!"

"Of course she won't agree! What wild thing has ever

agreed to be tamed? But tame her I will just as I tame my hawks.

"It's a most amusing process. Have you ever witnessed it? No? Well, the secret is to keep them on a short chain, hungry and confused. Oh, at first they flap and flutter all about in a futile effort to escape. But they soon learn to curb their tempers if they wish to eat. They soon learn their keeper's call and do his bidding.

"It's thus I'll tame the wild creature upstairs. Within three months she will bow to me as her Lord, her sovereign, her keeper, her husband. Katherine, the cursed shrew, will cease to exist. In her place will be Katherine the obedient, Katherine the quiet, the patient, the humble . . . ."

Philemon interrupted with a burst of raucous laughter. "I believe such fine brandy has pickled your brains, old man. Katherine the obedient, indeed! I'll wager you twenty ducats it can't be done."

"Twenty ducats? On a wife? I wager that much on my hawk or my hound or my horse. And the one upstairs is a rather fine horse, don't you agree? Of a good breed, at least. Just badly broken."

"One hundred ducats then."

"One hundred it is!"

Glasses clinked again as Katherine sat hunched into a ball on the cold marble floor of the library's antechamber. The floor felt as hard as her heart and her brain.

Meanwhile the two men's groggy conversation continued. "Well," said Cesaro, "my young friend, matchmaker, and soon to be brother-in-law, what say you to a quick trip to Venice? It's less than a day's ride from here. Lots of merriment there I could show you."

"Don't you want to spend time with Katherine before the wedding?"

"I'll spend time enough with the bitch after the wedding. So what say you, hey? Plenty of wine and women in Venice."

"Plenty of wine and women here."

"But the women in Venice won't insist on marrying us!"

Philemon, now befuddled from the brandy, found Cesaro's comments enormously amusing and laughed uproariously. Then he must have lost his balance and fallen for Katherine heard a great crash and the sound of crystal shattering.

Now both men seemed to lose control and, laughing even harder, they tried to quiet each other. Cesaro croaked, "I think we'd better get out of here before we completely wreck our future father-in-law's entire library. Come on, get up."

"Help me up," pleaded the giggling Philemon.

"All right, I'll help you up, you drunken sot, but I'm not going to carry you!"

The sounds of thumping and snickering continued in the room. But then, to Katherine's horror, the sounds became louder and closer. She suddenly realized that not only were the two men at last on their feet, but they were heading directly toward her. They apparently intended to exit by the back door through the antechamber where she hid, and not through the proper library door which led to the great reception hall.

She quickly scrambled to her feet, but it was too late. She could never make the hallway without being seen. The moment they passed through the archway they could not miss spotting her, even in their befuddled state.

She was trapped.

V

A FOUNTAIN
TROUBLED

But then, on the very verge of being discovered and humiliated, a rescuer appeared out of the darkness.

A small figure from behind her darted past her. Katherine, plastering herself against the common wall, watched in amazement as Matto positioned himself under the archway and barred the two men from passing through and discovering her.

Where had he come from? Had he been behind her the whole time while she had focused all her attention on the library? Had he, too, heard all that she had? Matto, claimed one serving girl who feared him, heard everything. He was a devil, the ignorant girl claimed. And now he had indeed appeared like a devil — but not to harm her. To save her.

"Gentlemen!" announced Matto in a voice deep and loud enough to penetrate the brain of the drunkest of revellers, "You'll disturb the other guests going this way. Come, I'll show you the way to your rooms." And, before they could object, Matto boldly took each of the startled men by an arm, turned them around, and led them through the opposite door.

As soon as Katherine was certain the way was clear, she ran out to the hall and bounded up the marble staircase two steps at a time. Reaching the sanctuary of her room at last, she slammed the door, blocked it with a chair, and then threw herself down onto the bed and buried her face in her pillow.

* * * * *

Beyond the villa's formal garden with its yew and cypress trees, its fountains and statues, was a small lemon grove. A twelve-foot stone wall sheltered it from the winter winds.

This was where Katherine chose to spend her time over the next few days. With a fur cape over her stiff brocaded gown, she hid from the masses of well-wishers in the villa and contemplated what she had learned that night in the darkness outside the library.

What sort of man, she thought, would place bets on the subjugation of his own wife? What sort of man would find triumph in his own wife's misery?

Not the sort of man, Katherine concluded, that she could ever marry.

But that was all that she could conclude. Katherine sensed she would have to make a decision soon — a decision that would change her whole life, a decision that, once made, would have irrevocable and unforgivable consequences. But she could not resolve what that decision was. The more she tried to grasp at an ideal solution, the more impossible it seemed.

And so she slipped into a curious passivity, curious in that for each day she delayed taking decisive action, the fetters of her future with Cesaro tightened even more around her. And the more they tightened, the harder it was for her to think clearly.

Already the wedding week entertainment had started. Moors performed torch dances at night. Clowns rolled and punched one another. Musicians and singers strolled the hallways while a Jewish dancing master taught the latest steps to men in satin waistcoats and women in velvet gowns.

Already five chests of fish, twenty marzipan cakes, and twelve dozen jugs of wine had been consumed. Her father was taking full advantage of the occasion to show his wealth and power to the whole Venetian Republic.

And the presents rolled in. Silks, satins, velvets, furs, tapestries, painted chests, jeweled caskets, crystal, bronze, silver, clocks, porcelain and jewelry. Ah, the jewelry! Gold crosses, rosaries of amethyst and pearls, bracelets, rings, headbands, and belts. Even in her despair, Katherine could not but be impressed by the bounty piling up in the reception hall. One gift in particular both amused and appalled her. A distant relative of her mother had sent her a wooden cradle, decorated with turquoise and gold, no doubt to remind her of the ultimate purpose of the wedding.

And upstairs, locked in a drawer in her room, Katherine kept the most expensive gift of all. Her parents had commissioned a necklace of large pearls with an almond-sized carved ruby set in a gold flower for her. This she was to wear on her wedding day.

The carnival atmosphere, the omnipresent wine and sweets, the gay music, the glittering and growing trove, the constant attention, all conspired to keep Katherine off balance. Only in the silence and solitude of the grove, under the grey winter sky with the dead leaves swirling at her feet, could she regain her perspective. There Katherine sat and remembered what all the pomp and fuss was leading to. And her heart and mind froze.

Three more days passed. And still she did nothing. Panic paralyzed her.

In the meantime, Cesaro and Philemon had returned from Venice only a bit worse for wear. So now Cesaro and Katherine bowed politely to each other whenever they passed, neither making any attempt to know the other any better. The enraptured Emogena and Philemon spent hours in each other's company, holding hands and whispering.

Cesaro spent hours appraising the wedding gifts.

On the Friday before the wedding Katherine rode Cybele

so fast and so recklessly that the frightened animal at last revolted, reared up, and threw her. Then, before Katherine could grab the reins, the horse bolted off. Katherine, out of breath, her riding jacket torn, her cap lost, and her hair falling over her shoulders, raised up on one elbow and cursed the poor animal. And then almost instantly regretted the uselessness of the curse. The uselessness of it all.

She did not bother to get up. She simply lay back on the cold hard ground and stared at the sky. She knew she could have been killed in the fall. Was that what she wanted? Was that the only answer for her? She closed her eyes and thought about death.

The clatter of hooves interrupted her thoughts. She opened her eyes.

Matto. Of course.

"Mistress," he gasped, breathing heavily from the strain of trying to keep up with her, "you may wish to kill yourself but I have no desire to die with you. Unless you agree to ride at a normal pace I will leave you here and you will have to walk back!"

At this threat from a servant Katherine's innate haughtiness resurged and she sat up. "Since when do you give me orders, dwarf?"

"Since you have become a madwoman," he retorted. He paused, then smiled coldly. "You see, I have kept my wits. Whereas you, it appears, have lost yours."

"Bring me Cybele!" snapped Katherine, irritated by such impertinence.

"For what reason? So you can try to kill her and yourself again? I thought your church forbade suicide."

"Matto, I am warning you, if you do not bring me my horse, if you do not obey me this instant, you will live to regret it!"

"As you are going to live to regret your obedience, Mistress?"

Katherine flushed. "What are you talking about?"

"I told you almost two weeks ago that there was one who could help you."

"Pere d'Amboise?"

"The priest? No," Matto spat, "your priest helps no one in Padua anymore. He has already left for Venice, from there to proceed to China, to Ethiopia, to Brazil, to only God and the pope know where.

"Ah, I see you have not heard of this yet? Well then, you can thank yourself for it. It seems he took your desertion of the faith to heart, Mistress Katherine. He saw he had failed you. He now seeks to make it up by teaching the concept of sin to innocent heathens."

Katherine shrugged at the news. "What do I care of him, he could not help me." And then she remembered. "But you, dwarf, told me you know someone else who could. Or were you making it all up? Who it is? Tell me," Katherine demanded, "tell me and I'll give you a whole necklace of coral beads against the malocchio, a whole chest of them!"

Matto smiled in triumph. He had won her attention at last. From high atop his horse he removed his hat with a flourish and bowed his head. "Why Mistress, 'tis I! 'Tis I who can help you as I helped you that night outside the library. 'Tis I who know the only way out for you. 'Tis I!"

And then his smile vanished. He lowered his voice. "But as I told you before, there is a price for such precious help. And it's much greater than a chest of coral beads.

"So think about it. I'll fetch Cybele and you think about it. Think about how much it's worth to you to challenge the gods and change your fate."

And off he trotted before she could say another word.

VI
THE WEDDING-DAY

Katherine's wedding day dawned cold and grey. The yard servants who swept the stairs and street quickly returned to the kitchen to warm their chilled bones. The house servants polished and dusted one final time. The stable attendants brushed and combed and decorated her father's finest team for the wedding carriage. The cooks, who had been up even before dawn, plucked, chopped, mixed, baked, roasted, and stirred. All preparations had to be completed before noon as none of the staff wished to miss the High Mass and wedding.

Later in the morning, hours after the servants had awakened, the guest stirred. Immediately their personal maids and valets brought them trays and laid out their finery and cajoled them to hasten their toilettes. Everyone, even nobles of the court, was expected to be at the church by noon.

Fidelia, who had been up with the servants, wore a gown of green silk shot through with gold and silver threads when she went in to check on her daughter's progress. To her satisfaction she found Katherine in the midst of a flurry of activity, being dressed and groomed with the same intensity as the ostlers in the stables were now decorating and grooming their four-legged charges.

With a clap of her hand Fidelia cleared the room of all but Katherine, Signorina Lupe, and herself. Noting that Katherine's breakfast tray had not been touched, she gestured to her, "Please sit, Katherine."

"Yes, mother," obeyed Katherine docilely in her cream silk underwear.

"Katherine," her mother began, "I know you have opposed this marriage . . ."

"It's all right, mother," interrupted Katherine. "I have accepted it."

"She has come to her senses at last," offered Signorina Lupe in explanation.

"Well, good." Her mother looked at her daughter, not without suspicion, but she could not read anything in her daughter's expression. She never could. Or maybe she had never tried hard enough. Since Katherine had disappointed her twenty years before by being born a girl, Fidelia had paid little attention to her.

"I have come to ask you if you know what marriage entails. I feel it my duty as a mother to inform you of certain . . . obligations of a wife. Do you know what I am speaking of?"

"Yes, mother. Signorina Lupe has told me," said Katherine, smiling sweetly to the Signorina.

"I quoted St. Paul to her, signora," explained the signorina. " 'Let women be subject to their husbands, as to the Lord; for the husband is head of the woman, as Christ is the head of the Church.' "

"Well, yes," said Fidelia, "that is true enough. But there is more to marriage than that. Tonight, Katherine, tonight I know certain events will occur which will come as a great shock to you. I know they were to me."

Katherine, disconcerted by her mother's embarrassment, broke in, "Mother, please, there is no need to say this."

"Then you know what will happen tonight?"

Katherine averted her eyes from her mother's. "Yes, I know what will happen tonight," she repeated very deliberately, very soberly.

What a strange daughter I bore, thought Fidelia. *First she's disobedient and raving, then for two weeks she walks around as if in a trance, and now she seems queerly alert and impatient.* Nerves, concluded Fidelia. Every bride is nervous on her wedding day.

"I will leave you to dress then. Remember your father will be in the carriage waiting for you at half past eleven. The rest of us will all be at the church."

"Yes, mother, I know."

And then Fidelia did something she had never done in Katherine's memory. She came over to her, placed her hand on Katherine's bare shoulder and laid her cheek against her daughter's. Katherine almost pulled back from the shock of it. Did her mother at last regret all the embraces ungiven, all the affection withheld? The tender scene lasted only a moment, then Fidelia withdrew, blinking rapidly. She turned to leave.

"Wait!" cried Katherine, wanting to speak but not knowing what to say. Desperate to connect again with her mother, Katherine searched about for a common link, something Fidelia would understand. Spotting the magnificent wedding necklace on her dressing table, she picked it up and let it dangle in the light between her two hands. She turned to her mother to show her appreciation. "Thank you for the present, mother. It's very beautiful."

Fidelia, proud of her impeccable taste, smiled at the compliment. "I thought you would like it. There's a companion piece to it that I'll give you upon your first born."

"My first-born son or first-born daughter?"

Fidelia looked astonished at the question. "Why, your first-born son, of course." And, smiling again, her duty accomplished, she left.

Katherine repeated to her mother's vanished form, "Of course."

As if reading her thoughts, Signorina Lupe said, "That is the way things are, Katherine, you can't change life."

Katherine shrugged, as if accepting her words, but to herself she thought, *Ah, but there is one life I can change.*

At her mother's exit all the maids and hairdressers fluttered back in and around the small room. When the dressing resumed, Katherine casually asked to no one in particular, "Has anyone seen Matto?"

"That one!" sniffed the signorina. "With all the guests in the house to be entertained he goes off and disappears. No one has seen him since Friday. With all this work to do! Your poor mother. Of course I never could see why she found him so entertaining. To me he has a malignant cunning quality about him. He's always popping up where you least expect it. Have you noticed, his eyes seem not quite human?" And she crossed herself as did the maids.

By half past ten Katherine was at last dressed. She wore a magnificent peach silk gown whose boned, fitted bodice dipped below her waist both in front and behind. Below the wide, square neckline she wore a liar to make her breasts seem fuller. Under the skirt she wore both a panier and a frame of whalebone hoops to swell out her petticoats and skirts and give the impression of great fullness. The hairdresser, using all his skill, had added other hair onto her own, then piled it all high on her head, powdered it, and wound pearls, flowers and ribbons through it. On her feet she wore two-inch white silk high heels so flimsy that she doubted they would last the one walk down the aisle and back. With her puffed hair and heels added on to her natural generous stature she towered over everyone in the room.

Finally, when every artifice that could be added had been added, including the wedding necklace, Katherine looked at her reflection in the mirror. She could not recognize herself.

But, remembering she was being watched, she thanked all those present and smiled at them. "You have all done a wonderful job. Now go, hurry, you want to get to the church early to get a good seat." The grateful girls barely hesitated before taking her advice and scurrying out the door.

Now she had to get rid of the signorina. "Signorina," she asked, "shouldn't you be getting on your way also?"

"Oh, there is plenty of time for me," answered the older woman as she stroked the ruffles of Katherine's skirt with a longing in her eyes.

No, there is not plenty of time! thought Katherine. In only forty-five minutes she was expected to meet her father at the entrance of the villa. Did Signorina Lupe suspect something? Katherine felt herself begin sweating under all the silk.

Five more minutes went by. And still the signorina did not leave her. Now she had only forty minutes before she was expected downstairs.

The great hallway clock ticked on. Five more minutes lost.

The villa grew silent around the two women. Everyone was either at the church or on his way to the church by now. Everyone but Katherine, Signorina Lupe, and her father.

Think of something! she ordered herself.

And at last the solution came.

"Signorina," Katherine blurted out so loudly that the woman started. "Signorina," repeated Katherine more quietly, "you must know how nervous I am. I should like to be alone before I meet my father. To pray, to ask for guidance. I'm sure you understand."

Signorina Lupe looked up at her. Katherine, in a near panic, first thought the woman was going to refuse. But finally the signorina smiled and got up.

"Of course my dear," she said. "I will see you at the church. Remember Katherine, the woman who pleases the duke controls the duchy. And the woman who rules the king rules the kingdom. Don't worry, Katherine, it will all be over soon."

"Yes, it will be," agreed Katherine, bending down so the diminutive signorina could kiss her on the forehead and bless her.

Katherine waited for the signorina's steps to disappear down the long tiled hall before she dared move. Now she had a new worry. Where was Matto?

Then, as if on cue, she heard a low knock at the door. Katherine ran to open it, dragged the little man in, then closed the door behind him and propped up a chair against it.

Matto, dressed soberly in traveling clothes, stood out in stark contrast to the bejeweled and beribboned Katherine. No scarves and baubles on him today. And no smiles either. He handed her a large package.

"I thought you would never get rid of her. We have less than half an hour. Hurry!"

"I'm trying to." But her gown, the pride of the dressmaker, must have had eighty buttons.

"Rip it," ordered Matto when he saw the problem.

She followed his orders and down to the floor fell the two-hundred-ducat gown and all its skirts and hoops. As Matto undid the torturous whalebone corset, she kicked off the ridiculously fragile shoes. At last, reduced to her shift, she tore open Matto's package.

"But it's so plain, so undistinguished," she complained without thinking as she held up the man's black suit before her.

"The more plain, the more anonymous," he answered. "Your safety — and mine — is going to depend on not drawing attention to yourself. Remember geese are plucked for their feathers. Do you want to get caught? And plucked?"

"I'm sorry. You're right, of course," apologized Katherine quickly. And with that apology began the start of a new relationship between them, one in which Matto gave the orders and Katherine obeyed them. Katherine quickly pulled on the pieces that went with the black suit, including the low-heeled sturdy black shoes that came with it. *How comfortable men's clothes were,* she thought. *How easily they allowed one to breathe and walk.*

Only the coiffure stood in the way of her metamorphosis now. Tearing through the stiff structure, she threw pins, ribbons, and pearls on the floor. Matto, she noticed, pocketed the ropes of pearls. When she had gotten most of the extraneous material out, she took up her scissors and started hacking away.

"Here, I'll do that, you sit down." He grabbed the scissors from her hand, and expertly began cutting through her thick brown hair. Even under all the pressure Katherine was amused as she watched the process in the mirror.

"You do that very well, Matto. Are you a barber as well as a jester?"

"I have many talents, Mistress. And we are going to need most of them if we are to succeed. There you are now, much better."

And there she was indeed. Once again she studied herself in the long mirror. But in place of the sacrificial virgin of a quarter hour before, a somber young man stood. A poor divinity student. A poor divinity student who wore a ruby necklace. Katherine hastily hid the beauty under her collar and appraised herself again in the mirror. For the first time in her life Katherine was grateful she did not have her sister's curves, nor her mother's delicate bones.

"Yes," she concluded. "You know I really think this scheme of yours might work."

"Good. It had better because there's no turning back now. Let's go! Have you the coin, the jewels, all you could find?"

"In the tapestry satchel, under the bed."

Matto retrieved the bag and briefly scanned the contents. "Good," he said again. "We're going to need every ounce where we're going." He turned. "Are you ready?"

"Yes."

"Then let's go."

Matto, carrying the satchels, removed the chair from Katherine's door and peered out. Katherine, right behind him, suddenly gave a small cry.

"I almost forgot," she explained. Running back to her chest she opened the bottom drawer. There, under a dozen pairs of silk shoes, she located the letter she had written the night before, unrolled it, and placed it on the bed.

And finally, with one last glance at the disarray behind her — the yards of torn peach silk, the curls of hair, the ribbons, the underwear — she threw a long black cloak around her shoulders and followed Matto out into the hall.

On the bed in which she would never sleep again lay a letter which read:

To Most Noble Excellent Signor, my father, and to my sweet illustrious mother,

You have done your duty by me as you saw fit. I have tried to do my duty by you. But I am unable to go through with this wedding.

So I am leaving.

I know, because of this deed, I shall never see either of you again.

I beg you to take care of yourselves.

I am sorry for all the distress I have caused you.

Kathleen Magill

I beg you most humbly to forgive me.

She had signed it,

> Your obedient daughter,
> Katherine.

But she had crossed out the word "obedient."

VII

A COLD WORLD

Near disaster stuck almost immediately after they left Katherine's room. A lowly kitchen maid, taking advantage of the absence of her superiors, rambled about the great public rooms, pinching bits of the elaborately laid-out delicacies and in so doing, effectively blocked the escape of the two conspirators. Matto, gesturing at Katherine to hide herself, stole up behind the girl and yelled "Caught you!" so loudly and unexpectedly that the poor terrified girl ran screaming from the room.

The way now clear, Katherine left her hiding place and joined Matto. When they passed the glittering tables of presents she saw him reach out to grab some treasure.

"No!" ordered Katherine in a harsh whisper. "If every one of those gifts is not returned to its proper giver my father will be even more disgraced." When Matto looked as if he would disregard her wishes Katherine added another explanation. "And if we cause him even more humiliation and shame, he will never cease pursuing us."

This logic, the logic of self-preservation, Matto recognized. So he moved on to the tables of food, filling every one of the twelve pockets of his cloak with hams, sausages, chickens, breads, and wines.

"Matto, we don't have time for this," Katherine complained.

"Mistress, I suggest you do exactly what I'm doing."

"I'm not hungry," snapped the exasperated Katherine as she watched him continue his pillage.

"Maybe not now, but I promise you will be later. No regular meals where we're going."

So, just to hurry him on, she acquiesced and stuffed some sweetmeats and cheeses into her pockets, and threw a bottle of brandy into her already stuffed satchel. Then they headed toward the terrace doors, the doors directly opposite the front gate where her father awaited her in his carriage.

The coast looked clear. Still, they could not hurry across the garden, for if someone were to be idly watching from the second or third story rooms, the sight of two fleeing figures with curiously bulging pockets would draw unwelcome attention. But the sight of a mere house servant strolling through the garden with a young guest would not be considered noteworthy.

They reached the far garden wall at 11:30, the exact time her father expected her to emerge from the opposite end of the villa. Katherine knew the wall before her well. As a rebellious child she had climbed it many times. She directed Matto to its lowest point and boosted him over. Then she threw over all the satchels and loose provisions, then scrambled over herself. The continuing ease with which she could move in pants amazed and pleased her.

Safely outside the wall, they proceeded to a nearby copse where Matto had concealed the horses. Matto had not stolen his usual gentle mount for himself, but a tall and powerful gelding instead. For Katherine he had brought the faithful Cybele. As she helped him mount he urged her to hurry.

"They'll sound the alarm soon. We've got to be well away."

And off they started with a gallop, neither looking back.

No longer was she Katherine Baptista; never would she be Signora Benno. The shrewish daughter of Ignatius of Padua was dead. In the small room in the great villa were her only remains — a dozen yards of peach silk and a fistful of thick brown hair.

But as one Katherine had surely died, another was surely born on that wild ride north in the cold winter sun.

It took them less than a quarter of an hour to reach the main highway to Padua and Venice. However, to Katherine's amazement Matto turned to the west. Pulling up Cybele, she shouted, "Where are you going?"

He stopped and shouted back, "To Genoa, of course."

"I thought we were going to Venice," said Katherine, pointing right, to the east. "It's only twenty miles to Venice. We can catch a ship there. It's got to be at least a hundred and fifty miles to Genoa — Genoa's all the way across the country, it would take us a week! Are you mad?"

"Are *you* mad?" he asked her. "I told you to leave the details to me."

"But why are we going so far out of our way?"

"You have a lot to learn, Mistress. Of course it is only natural to go to Venice. Of course Venice is the natural place to go. And once they determine you are not in Padua, where will they look? Venice. Naturally.

"Even if we found a ship immediately, with the quarantine in force, we would not be allowed to sail on her for ten days. You and I would never last ten days unnoticed. We would never last two days unnoticed, thanks to my stature and your demeanor. Besides, one of my rules when I'm in danger is to determine the obvious thing to do, and then do the opposite. Now come on!"

Katherine, seeing the merits of his argument as well as his determination, turned Cybele west and followed Matto.

All day long they rode at a steady pace, seeking to put as much distance between them and Padua as possible. Finally, just outside Verona as darkness fell, they found a greenwood on a hill which offered them a slight shelter from the wind. When Katherine at last dismounted, her knees buckled under her and she almost fell. Never had she ridden so long and hard. Because she could barely walk she gave up trying and simply sank to the cold hard ground and moaned. "Couldn't we at least stay at an inn?" she asked, huddling under her cloak and sucking on a smashed sweetmeat from her pocket.

"Not tonight," explained the dwarf. "We are too close to your father's friends and your intended husband's lieutenants for comfort. Tomorrow night. Maybe. Depends."

"On what? We certainly have enough money."

"Oh, do you wish to flash all your gold and jewels to strangers in strange places when you don't know what awaits you along the next curve? Or who awaits you along the next curve? Remember we are just student and servant. And I will handle all the money. You just try and look studious and poor. Don't talk to anyone. Don't do anything to draw attention to yourself. Don't be different from everyone else. Believe me, life is easier for those who can blend in, who can look and act like everyone else. People fear those who are different from themselves."

Even in her fatigue, Katherine recognized the shadow behind his words. "Do you think people fear you, Matto, because of your size?"

"Of course they do."

"And does that make you sad?"

"Oh no, Mistress Katherine," he grinned, changing the mood. "I have found it to be a great advantage. People fear me because they think I might have some powers they don't. Powers that made me so different from them. Dark, occult powers.

"And if people think you have power then, voilà, you do have power! It helps, of course, when I mention that my grandmother was one of the celebrated witches of Florence who trained me in the rites and beliefs of the Old Religion."

Katherine raised her left eyebrow.

"Oh, you do not believe me? But it's true. Ask any of the kitchen maids. I know many legends, many secrets. Would you like me to tell your fortune?"

Katherine thought it was all nonsense. "I would rather you tell me how I can possibly sleep on this cold rock we're on."

"If you're tired enough you can sleep anywhere." Then, noting her skepticism, he added, "So this is the first night you have not slept under the smooth sheets of a soft bed, hey?"

"Yes," she admitted, someone annoyed at his mocking tone.

"Well, it's not going to be your last until we're well out of this." Matto uncorked the brandy and handed it to her. "Here, take this and it will help you forget the hard ground and cold wind."

Katherine drank it straight from the bottle and it did indeed warm her. Then she passed it back to Matto who drank twice as much as Katherine had. And so they passed the evening, sharing brandy and bread until Katherine could no longer keep her eyes open.

The next morning Katherine awoke with the sensation of wetness on her face. Opening her eyes, she discovered that a fine winter rain had started and was rapidly soaking through her clothes. But she and Matto dared not take shelter from the storm. They had to keep moving.

And so they did what had to be done. For three days they sloshed through the countryside, facing and overcoming thunder, lightning, overflowing streams, and mud roads in which the horses became mired. To rest, to sleep, to be warm, clean and dry, that was all Katherine wished for during those miserable three days.

Finally, when they reached Milan, the sun broke through at last. And at last they rested. When Matto disappeared for half a day to sell some of her jewelry Katherine took the opportunity to tour the city on her own. Delighted with the mobility her disguise gave her she, for the very first time, tasted coffee — a drink which her father had forbidden her as "too stimulating for a lady." And, although warned by Matto to speak to no one lest her voice reveal her secret, she found she could get along quite well with simple gestures and monosyllable grunts. She acted as if she wanted to be left alone, and so she was.

She strolled the streets and galleries unattended, she entered bookshops and leafed through whatever volume she wished, not just those deemed "fit for ladies' eyes." She thrilled in the freedom of anonymity.

She was happier than she had ever been.

There was no going back for her now, even if a way had been miraculously presented to her. For she had tasted freedom. And she could not give it up. By the time they were ready to continue their journey, even Katherine's body reflected the changes in her life. She breathed deeper, stood up straighter. Her skin glowed from being outside all day. And after over a week of either erratic meals or none at all she had lost most of her pudginess. As her features sharpened, so did her mind.

The well-traveled road from Milan to Genoa offered none of the obstacles of the previous highway. They now rode steadily, comfortably for they felt as if they were no longer fleeing from something, but fleeing to something.

Both Katherine and Matto paused automatically when they finally reached the hill overlooking the port city. The two odd companions gazed at all the ships resting in the glittering sea, ships with bare masts that formed a grotesque swaying forest. These ships represented all the wealth of choices available to them.

Neither Katherine nor Matto spoke. But they shared the same thought, a thought also shared by so many other bold souls who chose to go adventuring: *Surely one of those ships will take me away to a wonderful land where everything is different, where all my problems will disappear, where I will find perfect happiness.*

And, if not, I'll just find another ship.

VIII
ON THE SEAS

Within two days Matto had found them an argosy, the *Mag Mell*, a three-masted square-rigger out of Liverpool. She was bound for the English colony of Virginia via Marseille, Madeira, and the Canary Islands.

Matto made all the arrangements, telling Katherine merely to stand up straight and keep her mouth shut. The latter advice was unnecessary for although Katherine knew Greek, Latin, French, and Spanish, she knew little English. She soon gave up trying to follow the conversation so she let her attention wander over the bustling deck.

On her one trip to Venice she had seen ships from afar but she had never been on one. She was surprised at how small the *Mag Mell* was; it was not even as long as the villa's reception room. And on this small assemblage of wood and nails they were to cross the vast ocean?

The powdered and bewigged English captain transacted the details of their passage with hardly a glance at Katherine and with a barely concealed disdain for Matto. However, the crew, in contrast to the captain's disinterest, frankly stared and pointed at the odd duo. *Perhaps,* thought Katherine, *they did not have dwarfs in England.*

When back on shore, Matto told Katherine he had signed them on as Signore Antonio Baptista and Servant. Captain Burgess, he said, was not pleased to hear of "Signore Baptista's" intended profession for he feared any "papist bull" contamination of his ship. "But I assured him that you were only a novice, a scholastic, sent abroad by your noble family because you had questioned your calling.

"I promised him you would not try and convert his crew. I even hinted that perhaps you were ripe for conversion yourself. Oh, that made his eyes light up. Watch men's eyes, Mistress, er," Matto caught himself, "Master, and you will learn many things from them. There is more knowledge in men's eyes than in books."

"And what else should I learn?" asked Katherine as they walked toward the marketplace where Matto insisted they purchase their own food for the voyage. Matto claimed that all ships' food was infested with maggots.

"First," he said, "you should learn to listen more than you speak and to remember what you hear. And whenever you get a chance to learn anything new, whether a language or a skill or a trick or a dance, learn it. You never know what might save your neck some day. But even when you're learning, you must keep your distance. No one must suspect you are not what you say you are. No one must suspect what lies under your clothes, and what lies you tell to keep your secret. No one. You are now Master Antonio Baptista not only to those sailors back there but to the whole world ahead of us.

"Act as if you know what you are doing and others will believe it."

Katherine smiled and didn't believe it. "Anything else?" she asked.

"Yes. Trust no one and always smile as if you know great secrets."

With a raised eyebrow Katherine looked down at Matto and noticed that that was the very smile he carried on his own face. So Katherine mimed the mime and smiled likewise.

On Friday the *Mag Mell* sailed with the tide. The great white sails fluttered and filled in the wind as the officers shouted to the sailors and the sailors ran to obey. Katherine stood by the rail out of the way on the upper deck, watching everything and speaking to no one just as Matto had advised. Not that anyone tried to speak to her. After all, she was a "furriner," a member of the Italian nobility and always accompanied by that "queer little fellow." Besides, everyone else aboard was too busy. Until they reached the open water of the Atlantic, tight navigation precluded any leisurely conversations.

Katherine and Matto watched as, slowly, the coast of Italy disappeared. Katherine was not sad, she felt no particular bond for her native land. For her birthplace maybe. For Venice maybe. But prior to 15 days ago, that was all she had ever seen of the country. She had never been to Rome. She had never been to Florence. Matto claimed they were both full of English tourists. Well, now she would see far more than Rome and Florence.

Matto interrupted her thoughts. "The cook tells me that there are many pirates between Genoa and Marseille."

"Pirates?" questioned Katherine.

"Maltese pirates mostly. And Barbary Coast ones. But, he claims, they only attack the Turks and Greeks, not the English. The threat of England's powerful navy has put a stop to attacks on her ships in the Mediterranean."

"Is that why you chose an English ship, Matto? Are you afraid of pirates?" Katherine teased.

"Aren't you?"

"I don't think they exist anymore. I think all the stories are exaggerations, nighttime tales made up to frighten children into good behavior."

"There's truth behind a lot of nighttime tales, Master Antonio."

"Perhaps," shrugged Katherine. "But why should you concern yourself if they don't attack English ships?"

"I said only that Maltese pirates don't attack English ships in the Mediterranean. But there are pirates other than the Maltese and seas other than the Mediterranean."

With the deck rolling beneath her feet and the sea breeze moistening her face Katherine was too exulted to share his consternation. "You worry too much, Matto," she chided. "You forget most of our worries are over." As the wind whipped through her hair, she smiled at him. "No one can catch us now. We have made good our escape. A wonderful future awaits us. I will never forget the great service you have done me. Without your help, I know I would not be standing here now, I would not be heading for a new land, I would not be free. The worst is over. Now we can relax!"

"Your innocence terrifies me," responded Matto. "More than pirates do."

For the next three weeks Katherine followed Matto's advice and observed and learned. She learned enough English to carry on simple conversations with the captain and officers. She learned something of the mysteries of navigation, of tides, winds, waves, currents, and quadrants. Being already skilled in mathematics and astronomy, she easily assimilated the new knowledge. Even the grim and autocratic Captain Burgess was impressed by his young passenger's aptitude. "Most passengers," he told her, "couldn't tell the North Star from the North Sea. And couldn't care either. Perhaps you've found a new calling."

And perhaps she had. For Katherine did love the salt spray flying, the gulls crying, the sails groaning and straining. She especially loved the scary freedom of being out of sight of all land. Most new passengers were terrified when they lost sight of land and when the wind blew and the waves rose. But not Katherine. She was exultant.

At Madeira, the *Mag Mell* was loaded with hundreds of

barrels of wine and stronger spirits to exchange later for Virginia tobacco and Jamaican molasses. But none of the crew was allowed ashore to take advantage of Madeira's most famous export. "Because," explained third mate Tom Tyrell, "a true sailor never stops with just one drink or two. A true sailor drinks only to get drunk. And when drunk, every sailor considers himself equal to a prince, or to a king, or even," Tom said, lowering his voice, "equal to a captain."

"Is that why you did not wait for a good wind before setting off?"

"No. The captain follows the old precept, 'He that will not sail till he have a full fair wind, will lose many a voyage.' "

Katherine nodded, understanding. She liked this somber, young, blue-eyed third mate. He talked to her as if she were his peer. Of course, he didn't know she wasn't.

One day when he joined her at dusk as she was leaning over the rail watching the white-capped waves, he began to speak of the changes he would like to make in shipboard procedure.

"When you are captain of your own ship," she comforted him, "you will be able to make all the changes you wish."

But instead of cheering him, her words seemed to increase his melancholy. "That will never happen," he told her. "The English believe that the paramount requirement for a command is to be born a gentleman. Like you."

Katherine turned away. Sometimes her deceit made her uncomfortable.

"I, Signore Baptista," he confessed, "am the son of a grocer."

Katherine, well aware of the rigidities of class, particularly since she herself had so benefitted from them, thought of a solution. "Could you not marry to improve your class?"

Tom Tyrell gave a short, bitter laugh. "I did," he told her. "I married the daughter of one of the merchants who owns this ship. That's the only way I got this far."

"Well then," consoled Katherine, "he is certain to help the man who married his daughter. After all, you would not have been allowed to marry her in the first place without his approval."

"Oh, he approves of me all right. He himself pushed the marriage. His daughter, you see, is much older than I. I was her last likely prospect. In return for marrying her he promised me a position on one of his ships. I found out too late he only had one. And a rotting, rat-infested one at that. After the marriage I also found out he's in desperate financial straits. If this voyage isn't a success he'll be bankrupt. And then I'll be stuck with a wife I don't love and who doesn't love me, destitute in-laws, and no commission. And no hope."

The last rays of the sun had disappeared into the black sea but Katherine could think of no more words of comfort for the young man. Not so long ago she too had experienced hopelessness, so she knew how empty cheerful phrases could be.

"Good Lord," he exclaimed suddenly, "how I must be boring you with all my troubles. I'm so sorry. I guess your being a priest, or almost-priest, brings out the confessional spirit in me." Again he apologized, "I'm terribly sorry," and he turned to leave.

Katherine, laying a hand on his arm, restrained him. "Wait. Please don't go. I'm not bored. I just don't know what to say. And I'm not a priest, just a student. The only words of comfort I know to give you are that to tell you that I, too, was once in what seemed to be a hopeless situation. But I found a way out. And so might you."

Before they could continue their conversation, the second mate called him for the watch change.

"We will talk tomorrow, yes?" asked Katherine.

"Yes," promised Tom, "tomorrow."

IX
A NOBLE GENTLEMAN

But at dawn the next day, as the sun rose out of the sea, a small dot appeared on the horizon.

Another ship.

Growing ever larger, she seemed to be headed straight for the *Mag Mell*. Each officer took turns at the glass to try and fathom her out.

"Anyone recognize her?" Captain Burgess asked.

"No, . . . Not I, . . . Nay, . . ." and "She's a strange one, she is," was all he got in reply.

With his legs spread wide to keep his balance on the rolling deck, the captain quickly made a decision. Although just two days away from the safety of the Canaries, he ordered their course changed.

The strange ship altered hers in return.

"Damn!" The captain, who tolerated no foul language from any of his crew, swore. "Damn her body and soul, she's after us!"

He quickly checked the sails, the sky, and the wind. "She's faster than we are but she's leeward. She won't be able to fetch us up unless the wind changes. We've got a fine humming breeze on our side now but women and wind change in a moment. I don't care how far off course we have to go," he ordered, "don't let her get windward of us."

And so the day went. With each change in the wind, Captain Burgess ordered a corresponding change in course. But for all his considerable skill, he never could lose that ominous black dot trailing them.

"Why is Captain Burgess so worried?" Katherine asked Tom Tyrell at one point during that tense day. "Cannot this strange ship be a merchantman like us?"

"Why would a merchantman be chasing us?" was his reply.

"She flies a friendly flag doesn't she?"

"In the middle of an ocean, what's to prevent a ship from raising false colors? Would not a false ship bear a false flag?"

"So we are in a perilous situation?"

"Yes. 'Tis a good thing you're a man of religion, signore. If they do catch us and board us, they might have Catholics amongst their crew who might spare you."

Katherine clenched the rail, bewildered. "How could they board us? We are larger than they are!"

"But our gunports are false, theirs aren't. I count sixteen cannon on her. And pirate ships carry three to four times our crew." He paused, then lowered his voice and disclosed bitterly, "We were supposed to carry cannon, of course, but my father-in-law and his partners were too cheap to pay for the crew to man them, so he had the guns removed and sold."

"So if they catch us, we cannot fight them?"

"What would we have to fight them with? Madeira wine? French silks? Italian tiles?" He laughed humorlessly, then shook his head. "No, our only hope lies in escaping them during the night by drastically changing our course."

And that is precisely what Captain Burgess did. Sometime around midnight he turned northeast, although the Canaries lay due south of them.

Few aboard the *Mag Mell* slept that night. Katherine lay in a cold sweat on her narrow bunk and let her imagination run wild. She reviewed every horror story she had ever heard of pirates. Stories that she hadn't believed. Until now. Pirates, she remembered being told, enjoyed beating, mutilating and torturing their victims before murdering them. Pirates would tie a prisoner in front of a cannon and blow his head off for amusement. And if they found out she was a woman . . . why, pirates were known to do unspeakable things to women.

When she could not stand lying there along with her dreadful thoughts any longer, she got up and joined Matto and the rest of the crew on deck to shiver and await the dawn. They would not know if they had lost their pursuer until day-break.

The light had never seemed so long in coming. With excruciating slowness the black at last yielded to grey, and the grey to dark blue, and the dark blue to light. Forty-six pairs of eyes anxiously scanned the horizon.

And saw nothing.

They were alone in the vast grey ocean. When there could be no doubt of their fortune, the tension broke with the force of a gale wave. Forty-five men — and one woman — shook their heads and laughed and congratulated each other and slapped each other on the back in relief.

Captain Burgess came to the rail of the quarterdeck and looked down upon the jubilant crew on the deck below. "Well, gentlemen," he announced, "it looks as if we've lost her, God be praised."

"God be praised, and Captain Burgess be praised!" shouted back one sailor.

Captain Burgess acknowledged the tribute with a nod. Then he turned back to the helmsman and shouted, "Back on course, south to the Canaries!" And to the men below he shouted, "And a ration of rum for the hands, to drink to God and the great wind and sea for saving us!"

A great cheer rose up from the men below him. The captain, about whom the crew had groused since setting sail, was now a hero and a fine fellow for outwitting the pirates. A new ditty was sung throughout the day:

> Come all you sailors bold,
> Lend an ear, lend an ear,
> Come all you sailors bold, lend an ear:
> 'Tis of our captain's fame,
> Brave Burgess was his name,
> How he fought on the main
> The pirate bold, you shall hear.

"Well, captain," said Katherine to him when he strolled by her later that afternoon, "you certainly know how to change a man's tune. Until now, I thought sailors spent all their days complaining."

"Signore Baptista, I will tell you a secret of the sea," he responded. "Sailors always complain. Sailors always hate the captain and they always growl about him. Loudly. If a captain doesn't hear any grumbling, that's when he should start worrying. A silent crew is a mutinous one."

With that explanation, the captain started to move on, then abruptly stopped and turned back to her. "Would you care to join me tonight in my cabin for an after-dinner brandy?" he asked magnanimously. "I think we should hold a service of thanks tomorrow for our narrow escape and you, being a student of scripture, might help me find an appropriate text."

"Of course, captain," answered Katherine, "I would be honored."

And thus she found herself that very night sipping brandy from a crystal goblet in the captain's cabin.

The liquor and the release of tension made the proud old man talkative. On and on he ranted about how hard it was to command properly with such lower-class scum as he had aboard. "Ignorant fools and asses for the most part! Most can barely write their own names. Their thoughts revolve around cheap rum, cheap tobacco, and cheap women."

Katherine let him ramble on as they sat on opposite sides of the rich mahogany table which filled his room. She studied the plump pompous man in the queued wig before her and marveled. Dressed in a rich blue damask waistcoat and breeches trimmed with velvet, with a large emerald cross hung suspended from a thick gold chain around his neck, was this a man to tell what she had heard from Matto? Was this man aware of the multitudes of rats and cockroaches that infested the *Mag Mell*? Of the bilge water that had leaked into the lower decks from the heavy winter seas, sopping the men's clothes and blankets and giving them all the ague? Of the rotten meat and fish, the stinking drinking water? Of the first mate who was so free with his cane?

"Perhaps," she ventured, "the men are only ignorant out of lack of opportunity. Perhaps it is not their fault that . . ."

Before she could finish her sentence Captain Burgess scoffed and cut in on her. "I see their complaints have reached your ears. And you, being a well-born and gently nurtured man of God, you have taken their whining to heart. But you are young, you do not know the devious ways of most men, your cheek is still soft. You cannot understand the vulgarity, the innate coarseness of these men."

He looked at her through weary eyes for confirmation. "You want to save their souls, correct? Well, I am not adverse to saving their souls myself. If they have any. That's why I insist that every man jack aboard my ships attend my Sunday service.

"But I fear all my efforts go to waste. You have seen their attitude when I speak the Holy Word to them. Do they listen?

No! God to them is just a name to be called upon when the seas are rough. 'The danger past, God forgotten.' "

Katherine, who had attended his services along with everyone else, agreed that the men did not seem to take the captain's sermons to heart. But, she thought, why should they when the captain's usual text revolved around how they should all prepare for the devil's fire, how they should all, on the day of judgment, "go away into everlasting punishment"?

"Signore," continued the old man while pouring more brandy into their glasses, "I know your calling requires a certain sympathy for those less fortunate than ourselves, but I feel it my duty to warn you. Men below our station are dangerous. And that includes that servant of yours. To save their miserable skins they will turn traitor on you, on me, on their own mothers, and on God Himself."

Little did he know, as they sipped his best brandy, how soon his words would be verified.

X

A VERY FIEND

The next morning Katherine awoke to the sound of cannon. Almost immediately Matto burst into her cabin to tell her that the two-masted pirate brigantine, the *Taingire*, had trapped them. There was nothing Captain Burgess could do but heave to and let the cutthroats board his ship in hopes that, after they plundered his cargo, they would leave him, his crew, his passengers, and his ship itself unmolested.

With the officers isolated on the quarterdeck and Katherine, Matto, and the entire crew on the main deck, all watched in tremulous silence as the *Taingire* pulled closer and closer. When almost beside the *Mag Mell*, the *Taingire*'s heinous crew hurled grappling irons across the choppy water to make the two ships one.

The two crews faced each other as the lines were secured. One crew, the *Mag Mell*'s, watched mute and stock-still while the other's crew yelled and howled and whistled and jeered and laughed in great vile roars. They even had a drummer and trumpeter to add to the uproar.

Tom had been correct, the pirates outnumbered the merchant seamen by at least three to one. Katherine estimated their number to be over a hundred — over a hundred of the dirtiest, ugliest, foulest, roughest, scruffiest, vilest fiends she had ever seen.

Many were maimed, many were cankered, all were filthy. She could smell them before they even boarded. To add to her alarm, all carried or wore several arms, cutlasses, pistols, daggers, muskets, or axes.

The instant the two ships were latched together, a great cry of victory arose from the gleeful scum as they streamed across the *Mag Mell*'s deck, knocking down any who got in the way of their mad dash for bounty. Katherine, Matto and the *Mag Mell*'s crew were herded to the far rail and surrounded. Captain Burgess, Tom Tyrell, and the other officers were allowed to remain on the quarterdeck from where they watched the pillage in total helplessness.

Up came all the goods and stores from the hold: boxes, bales, cases, kegs. Soon silks, shirts, sugar, liquor, charts, navigation tools, even the officer's bedding were strewn all over the main deck. Fights broke out whenever two wretches claimed the same item. On the discovery of one particularly fine red brocade vest, the two claimants pulled great dirk knives on each other and might have drawn blood had not one tall dark-haired fellow brandished his cutlass and threatened them. As soon as they backed off he donned the red vest himself.

It took over two hours for all the goods to be divided up. The gold and jewels they had uncovered went into an urn they had placed in the middle of the deck. Most of the gold was from the Captain's strong box and Matto's poke, most of the jewels from Katherine's satchel. She was forced to watch what was to have been the foundation of her future stolen from her.

"This be all your gold and valuables?" shouted the one in the red vest to Captain Burgess as his cohorts stalked about, quieter now. And drunker.

Captain Burgess nodded coldly. "That be all."

"That be not much for a great merchant vessel."

"This be not a great merchant vessel," Captain Burgess replied. "This be just the *Mag Mell* out of Liverpool bound for the colonies with a load of wine and yard goods. And I be Wolcott Burgess, captain of her and her crew of worthy and god-fearing men."

The tall one grinned impudently. "And I be Brian Christopher, captain of the *Taingire* and her crew of desperate and god-cursing men!"

His men hooted in agreement. A few with bottles used his words as grounds for raising a toast and drinking. The pirate captain continued his threats. "Now Captain Wolcott Burgess, your Lordship, if I should find you or any of your men to be trying to hide any valuables from me and my men, I'll see this deck red with your blood. And I expect you to answer truly to all such questions as I shall put to you, otherwise you shall be cut to pieces."

Katherine thought of the necklace under her shirt. And of the few other jewels she had managed to secret in the inside pockets of her cloak. It was all she had left. As she had watched the pirates fussing over all brightly colored garments earlier, she silently thanked Matto for insisting on her plain black apparel. In the chill winter wind, a man wearing a cloak should be no cause for suspicion.

" 'Tis a fine morning, hey your Lordship?" Christopher declared. "A mild swell, a brisk wind, the sun shining, a day a sailing man lives for. And you're quite a sailing man, Captain. You gave us a good chase there yesterday. I bet you even thought you lost us. Well, you might of were you a free man like I.

"But you are skipper of a merchantman and merchantmen have schedules and ports they have to call. And where else would you be heading in this part of the great ocean but to the Canaries? All I had to do was wait off their coast, you were bound to return to your original course sooner or later.

"But I do admire the way you handled yourself yesterday.

I could use a man with your navigational skills. Would you care to join up with us?"

Captain Burgess kept his expression immobile as stone.

"No, I guess you wouldn't at that," said Christopher. "I can tell by your eyes that you're a righteous man, not one to traffic with the likes of us. But I'll bet for all your righteousness you've skippered plenty of slavers in your time."

Abruptly Christopher spun around and turned his back on Captain Burgess. "Line them up!" he ordered his men. So his crew jabbed and pushed the *Mag Mell*'s into a long, straight line. Katherine and Matto stood together near the end of it. Then, with slow deliberation, Christopher started walking down the length of it, pausing in front of each man to eye him up and down.

When he reached the man called Chippy, Christopher grabbed hold of his scarred hands, studied them and demanded, "You the carpenter?"

Chippy nodded.

"You're coming with us then, we need a carpenter."

As the unfortunate Chippy was pulled away from his mates he started to resist and object. "But, but . . ." was all he managed before Christopher cut him off with, "No buts! It's been duly noted that you're coming under protest and you can testify to that effect if we're ever caught and brought to trial. But in the meantime, just think, you'll have a share of that."

Christopher pointed to the urn with its glittering treasures. "That's probably the first time you've ever seen more than ten pounds in your entire life, isn't it? Stick with us and you might see hundreds, thousands more."

With that enticement, Christopher turned and addressed the whole line of *Mag Mell* prisoners. "Well, anybody else wish to join us and make his fortune? You'll never make it working a merchantman like this.

"Now, here's what I need. I need someone who knows navigation, who can read the stars and keep a steady course, I need gunners, and I need a cook."

When he got no volunteers, he continued his inspection. Katherine prayed to God that he would pass her by without notice but, to her horror, when he stopped in front of her he grabbed her smooth hands up into his rough ones. "These are not the hands of a sailor. What be your business on this ship, laddie?" he demanded with eyes as grey and cold as the sea surrounding them.

He clenched her hands so tightly that, in the pain, she at last found her voice. "I am a student."

"Of what?"

"Of God."

With that, he threw down her hands and cursed. "You're a damned baby priest, that's what you're saying. We at sea don't like priests, laddie."

Desperate to escape his wrath, she stammered, "I am not a priest, I'm a scholastic. To be a priest requires nine more years of study than I've had."

Her feeble attempt to assuage his anger didn't work. "Study of what?" he raved. "Of how to grab what's not yours and call it God's will?" Then he suddenly put both his hands on her shoulders and shook her, which compounded her fright. "It's not too late for you. Why don't you study something useful? Like medicine. Now if you were a student of medicine I could use you. You know anything about medicine?"

Katherine dropped her eyes and shook her head, terrified he would slit her throat just because he didn't like her and couldn't use her.

But, instead, with a final shake, he dropped his hands

and simply turned away.

She was saved. She would live.

But now he stood in front of Matto. "And you, dwarf, do you know anything of use?"

"I know a great many things of use," piped the ever-boastful Matto. Katherine groaned to herself. Surely the clever Matto should know to keep his mouth shut in this perilous situation. Katherine had seen him act the simpleton before, if he would only act that role now, he would be ignored. And saved. But Matto didn't keep his mouth shut.

"Such as what?" asked the pirate captain Christopher. "What do you know that would be of value to me?"

"I know what herbs will take away fever. I know how to use that brandy that you're spilling over the deck to make a chicken taste like ambrosia, for I've been in plenty of noble kitchens, learning from witches and women. I know how to read the future in a deck of cards. I know over two hundred songs."

Then Matto paused and looked Christopher squarely in the eyes. "And I know that some day you'll all hang."

Christopher, who had seemed amused at Matto's words until his final ones, grabbed the back of the smaller man's collar and pushed him across the deck to stand with Chippy.

"If we hang, you'll hang too, dwarf!"

Katherine gave an involuntary cry as Matto fell amongst the marauders. Quick as a flash, Christopher whirled back to her. "What is the dwarf to you?"

"He is my servant," she replied.

"A servant who has not learned to keep his mouth shut."

"Please don't take him!"

"Ah padre, but he admitted himself that he can cook. And I need a cook."

"He did not mean it."

"Then why did he say it? I think, padre, you do not know your servant very well, not one-tenth as well as he probably knows you. Now, I know a smart man when I see one. I know your servant's smart enough to realize that he's better off with me than with you. After all, I've got the gold. You haven't."

Strolling to the middle of the deck, Christopher addressed Matto loudly enough for all to hear. "Well, dwarf, this useless priest boy thinks you join us unwillingly. What say you to him?"

"My master is . . . ," Matto began to answer when he was immediately interrupted by Christopher.

"Now that you are one of us, no man is your master, least of all one as useless as he."

"The youth is not useless," said Matto. "He has many talents too, but he is too modest to state them."

Matto, what are you doing? thought Katherine. *Stop talking!*

But Matto continued on. "The young lad can read the stars, can speak and write five languages, can play the harpsichord and lute . . ."

"A musician!" cried a voice from the back of the pirate mob.

"Take him!" cried another.

"Yes," agreed Christopher, "we could use another musician. We have two trumpet players and a drummer and they suffice well enough in battle, but we could use some variety. Well, padre, I guess you're not as useless as I thought. You're hereby recruited. And you can think your ex-servant for it!"

With those words he smiled, pulled Katherine out of the line and shoved her toward the other two *Mag Mell* "recruits." Katherine could not believe what was happening to her. She could not trust herself to look at Matto. Matto, who had saved her so many times, had now betrayed her. And for what? Gold? As soon as the pirates boarded, the gold was lost to him whether he left on the *Taingire* or stayed on the *Mag Mell*. So why did he deliberately contrive to have her join him?

Why did he doom them both?

XI
MONSTROUS VILLAIN

By the time Christopher reached the end of the line, three more unfortunates had been chosen to join Katherine, Matto, and Chippy.

"All right, now," announced Christopher as he started back down the line, "for those of you who are left, I'll give you a sample of pirate justice. Every man of us here knows full well the tyranny a poor sailorman puts up with. I'll bet there's not one of you who hasn't been flogged, or caned, or knocked about unfairly.

"So if any of you has a grievance against any of the men standing up there on the quarterdeck, here's your chance to get even. Give us your evidence and we'll lash him to the capstan for you and let you take whatever revenge you choose."

Katherine could see the sudden glints in some of the *Mag Mell*'s crew's eyes. No doubt they were remembering past injustices from one or more of the four men on the quarterdeck.

"Captain Christopher," shouted Captain Burgess, one of the four potential targets. "I've had about enough of you. Now, you've taken everything aboard but what was bolted down and maybe you've even taken that. But you haven't harmed anyone yet. And let me warn you, if you should bring harm to any of the English patriots aboard this ship, England will avenge us. Remember, England has a great navy!"

"England also has great merchants who will supply me with all I need to escape her great navy," replied Christopher with a shrug. "Besides, why should I wish to escape her great navy when I sailed for her myself! How do you think I learned my trade?

"It was during the War of the Spanish Succession it was. I started out under Rogers privateering for Queen Anne herself by official government letter of marque. For which service I received public thanks. That service, I might add, consisted of doing just what I'm doing now. Looting ships. But only French and Spanish ones.

"Nothing quite like patriotic service, is there? Especially when one can pocket a profit from it.

"But back to the subject at hand. It's time, your Lordship, to take the secret vote of your crew to find out who lives and who dies. One advantage of being at sea, you know, you never have to bother with digging a grave now, do you?"

"May the sharks have his body and the devil his soul," chanted the men as the remains of the first mate's bloody corpse was tossed over the side.

The *Mag Mell*'s crew, taking Christopher at his word, had voted to avenge every lash, every blow, every humiliation the first mate had ever meted out. So on their behalf the pirates had forced the mate to circle around the mizzenmast during which they beat him every step of the way with whatever was handy — clubs, broken bottles, and flats of swords.

Katherine, sickened, tried to turn her back to the gory spectacle and blot out the sight of the man's agony and the blood lust in his tormentors' eyes from her mind. But she could not block the sounds of the victim's cries nor the derisive drunken laughter that greeted each scream. Katherine felt herself in the midst of a nightmare, a nightmare which would not soon end for, thanks to Matto, she was condemned to live with these savages for God knew how long.

For she saw now how there was no escape at sea except in death.

As soon as the mate's body disappeared under the waves Christopher began the final order of business, the transferring of the plunder from the *Mag Mell* to the *Taingire*.

"I would take your ship, too, Captain," Christopher said to Captain Burgess, "but your hull is rotten with worms and you've even more rats than we have, so you can keep her. Maybe, if you bail her 'round the watch, she'll float long enough for you to be rescued."

Above their heads a group of Christopher's men were stripping the *Mag Mell*'s masts of her sails and rigging. These, along with the liquor, the trade goods, the provisions, the bins of live pigs, goats and chickens, were all casually tossed over the railings to the deck of the *Taingire*. Only the urn of gold and jewels merited careful handing until safely stowed below the brigantine's decks.

Matto, now on the deck of the *Taingire* with Katherine and the other recruits, had already begun playing the role of cook. To all the cutthroats he promised a mighty feast that night. He calculated that such a gesture would earn him a secure position among them for he recognized from their sallow complexions that they had been at sea for weeks without proper rations. They would be overly satisfied with even the most rudimentary evidence of culinary skill.

Katherine watched as Matto chose several chickens from the fowl bins, strangled them, and started plucking. Then he startled her by throwing one at her and ordering her to start plucking along with him.

She turned away and refused to acknowledge him. Suddenly she felt him behind her, his breath in her ear. "Make yourself useful to them!" he hissed, forcing the bloody chicken into her hands. "Give them a reason, any reason, to keep you alive. Or do you want to end up like the first mate?"

Katherine looked around herself and saw several of the *Taingire*'s crew eyeing them suspiciously. Without a word, she sat down cross-legged on the deck and started plucking. *I'll make myself useful all right,* she thought. *I'll make myself so useful that no one will dare to lay a finger on me. I will live through this!*

From her little corner of the deck she glanced back over at the *Mag Mell*. The sight appalled her. She was a denuded hulk — no sails, no ropes, no compass, no quadrant. And no first mate.

Captain Burgess, the second mate, and Tom Tyrell had still not moved from their places on the quarterdeck. Watching the frenzy of activity as the last of their goods and stores disappeared over to the *Taingire*, Captain Burgess's face had the frozen wrath of God about it, the second mate's face lacked any color at all, and Tom's face . . . well, Tom's face alarmed her. His eyes seemed too bright and his breathing too quick, and he was clenching the railing so tightly that his knuckles had turned white. Katherine felt almost as sorry for him as she did for herself. Both of us have lost almost everything, she thought.

But then, just as the pirates were about to detach the grappling irons that held the two ships fast together, Tom suddenly cried, "Oh God!" and ran down the stairs to the railing by the *Taingire*. "Captain Christopher!" he called out.

Christopher turned to face the young officer. All others fell silent.

"Captain Christopher," shouted Tom across the two railings, "you said you needed a man skilled in navigation."

Christopher carefully nodded.

"I'm that man."

"Mr. Tyrell!" boomed out the voice of Captain Burgess

above them, "Think what you be doing man!"

But Tom had apparently already thought enough. The success of the *Mag Mell*'s voyage was his only hope for a future; that hope had just been destroyed before his eyes. He had nothing to lose by joining the pirate crew. Nothing except his life.

"Come aboard then," shouted Christopher with a triumphant leer.

All watched as Tom leapt over the two railings and walked over to Christopher. Christopher, clapping him on the back, announced to those around him, "You shall be my quartermaster."

Upon hearing those words one of the men, a large, bushy-eyebrowed wretch, turned and glowered at Christopher. The man held one end of a freed grappling hook in his hands and looked fully capable of throwing it at Christopher at that instant. But, as Katherine watched the tense exchange, the man merely locked eyes with Christopher and muttered, "You son-of-a-whore," and walked away.

With the removal of the last grappling iron, the two ships shuttered, creaked, then parted. "Mr. Tyrell," shouted Captain Burgess, unable to resist one last warning, "this means you'll hang with the rest of them when they get caught!"

Tom Tyrell said nothing, just watched. Captain Burgess, realizing it was too late, seemed to soften. "Do you have any messages for your wife and father-in-law?" he yelled across the ever-widening gulf between them.

To the old man on the foundering *Mag Mell*, Tom shouted four words:

"Tell them I'm dead."

XII

GREAT GOOD CHEER

Matto did fix a proper feast that night, just as he had promised. Into the giant caldron went chicken, pork, corned beef, ham, olives, onions, garlic, mustard seed, salt, red wine, cognac, and every spice he could find. The famished crew descended upon Matto's concoction like greedy pigs, bolting down each bowl, then, smacking their lips, they belched and came back for more.

Katherine had no time to think for she had been pressed into stirring and ladling out the salmagundi in the middle of the open deck. All the cooking and celebrating had to take place in the open despite the chill wind for no smoking or fires or candles were permitted belowdecks. But after two casks of rum, innumerable bottles of claret and French brandy, most of the hundred-odd cutthroats were both blind to the weather and to everything else.

The celebrating, which began as soon as the *Taingire* was alone in the open seas, continued after sunset. During the long night of revelry the trumpeter and drummer played lively music and jigs that their cronies could dance and stomp and sing to:

> And let us be jolly
> and drown melancholy;
> And drink to the health
> of each black-hearted soul.

Getting progressively drunker, the men found it harder

and harder to dance on the rolling deck. Indeed, they found it harder and harder to even walk on the rolling deck. One by one they passed out.

To save them from tumbling off the deck into the surrounding black sea, the remaining few still able to maneuver dragged those now lifeless lumps of flesh over to an open hatch and dropped them in. By midnight, Matto, too, had disappeared down the hatch. All but a hardy half dozen lay snoring and scratching down below.

The party was over.

For the first time since dawn Katherine sat down, leaned back against a crate, drew her cloak and cap tightly around her, and gave in to her fatigue. She was too tired to think, too tired even to care about the morrow. With eyes closed she breathed in great gulps of the biting sea wind in a futile attempt to obliterate the pervasive stench of stale food, liquor, and unwashed bodies that clung about her and the *Taingire*.

When she at last opened her eyes she spotted, through the misted lantern light, the lone figure of Tom Tyrell at the helm. In some ways, she thought, he's worse off than I am. So, tucking a bottle of wine under her arm, she poured out a bowl of the remainder of the stew and started across the deck to him.

Tom had been at the helm for seven hours straight, keeping apart from the celebration, keeping alone with his thoughts. Having neither eaten nor drunk since daybreak, he gratefully accepted Katherine's silent offering. When she indicated she would relieve him at the wheel, he did not object.

She watched as he wrapped both his hands around the ceramic bowl to draw its warmth to his near frozen fingers. Sinking down to the deck, he rested his back against the rail and ate.

Neither spoke.

When he had finished the food he uncorked the wine she had brought and, slowly and deliberately, he started drinking. When he was halfway through the bottle, Katherine finally spoke.

"Why did you do it?"

He did not seem surprised at the question. He looked her straight in the eyes and simply stated, "How could I have gone back home in that wasted hulk in which so many of my hopes died?"

"But none of it was your fault."

"What does that matter? The deed was done. My doom was sealed."

And mine, thought Katherine.

"This seemed my only alternative. I was left with nothing."

"You have a family," she reminded him.

"Whom I care nothing about and whom I can do nothing for except go to debtor's prison."

"No!" He shook his head, denying them, and explained. "Alone, my conniving wife just might scheme her way out of this. She'll claim innocence, blaming her father, blaming her mother, blaming me, blaming the vicissitudes of fortune with such passion that the court is sure to show mercy. She's better off without me." The young man paused, then added, "No. There is nothing for me in England any more."

"Is there anything for you here?" Katherine asked.

"I have always heard pirates share their bounty equally amongst themselves."

"And I have always heard," responded Katherine, "that they share the rope equally, too."

Before Tom could reply, both he and Katherine were startled by the sudden bellow of a loud, rough baritone:

"Ah, 'tis true! 'Tis true what you both be saying!"

Up to the helm from behind a water casket reeled Christopher. Katherine had assumed he had passed out with the rest. From the quantity he had drunk he should have been at the bottom of the debauched pile in the hold. She wished he were there for his appearance still frightened her. He was such a dark man, black hair and beard . . . even his skin was dark, burnt deep red from the wind and weather. And yet, in the midst of that darkness were those light grey eyes, as piercing as a stiletto and as cold as the steel of one. Those were the eyes that shrewdly assessed the two before him before speaking again.

"Glad to see you two sharing a bottle. I won't have any goddamned puritans aboard my ship. Why, a sailor needs rum more than he needs clothes. For a tall enough glass will keep him warm in the cold and cool in the heat." Christopher smiled as if to show amiability but his eyes reflected ice in the swinging lantern light.

Christopher seemed to feel like talking and as it was his ship, both Katherine and Tom were smart enough to let him. "Now, as to what you were saying, it's true we share. We've got all the details of it set down in the *Articles*. We've all signed them. You'll have to sign them, too. Tomorrow. Nobody sails aboard the *Taingire* unless he signs them and swears on a Bible that he'll obey them."

"Just what are these *Articles*?" asked Tom guardedly.

"The standard ones," replied Christopher. "About each man having a vote and that sort of thing. That's how I got to be captain. I was chosen to be captain by vote and, according to the *Articles*, I could be voted out. But just let one of them try to vote against me, I'll slit his traitorous throat."

"What else?" asked Tom with even more caution after Christopher's last words.

"Let's see. There's one about marooning. And one about

what you'll get if you're maimed or crippled. And there's a couple about gambling and fighting and stealing. My personal favorite, of course, is the one about compensation.

"The captain and quartermaster — that's you, now, Tyrell — are to receive two full shares of a prize; the master, mate, doctor — although we don't have one at the moment — carpenter, boatswain and gunner are to have one share and a quarter. The rest split the remainder evenly. And every man regardless of rank gets an equal share of all liquor and provisions as long as they last. There's no brandy for the officers and bilge water for everyone else aboard a pirate ship!

"So you see, Tyrell, you made a smart decision back there. Next prize we catch, you'll get a share equal to mine. That's more than you'd ever make as a third mate on a moldy merchantman!

"Oh, just one more thing, though. If I were you, I'd steer clear of the one called Bucko, the big hairy fellow with the slit nose. He's a mean bastard and until today he was my quartermaster. He's not likely to fancy losing that extra share."

"Anything else I should know?" Tom asked coldly.

"Let's see . . . have I forgotten anything? Oh yes, there is one more thing. But if you're the kind that likes young boys like the lad here it's not an article you'll ever need concern yourself with. It's the one about how any man who tries to carry a woman to sea disguised shall suffer death.

"That's all."

Katherine tried as hard as she could to keep her expression neutral. Once again, the accident of her sex had placed her at the the edge of an abyss. She swallowed and tried to gather enough courage to speak. Finally the words came out. "What if," she asked Christopher, "we don't sign these *Articles*?"

"Ah, then, laddie, we'll just take a vote and decide on a fit punishment for such ingratitude. The men generally pick those punishments that result in lots of blood."

Tom and Katherine exchanged glances. "Of course we'll sign the *Articles*, Captain," Tom quickly replied for both of them.

"I thought you might," said the satisfied Christopher. Then he turned his attention to Katherine. "Now padre, I'd like to hear some music out of you. What did you say you played?"

"Harpsichord and lute."

Christopher contemptuously barked at her, "What did you think, that we carry a harpsichord aboard?" Then he paused, thought, and added, "Although we might pick up a lute somewheres, especially if we get us a Spaniard."

Katherine was tired of being yelled at and tired enough to talk back to him. "I did not ask to come aboard your ship, Captain," she reminded him.

"True enough. But you gave me the impression you'd be of some use to me."

Exhausted and irritated she snapped, "I gave you no such impression! Why would I want to be of any use to the likes of you?"

Christopher's eyes flashed at her scornful manner. Swift as a cat he drew his dagger from his belt, came up behind her and pinned her against the wheel with his left arm while his right hand flashed the knife in front of her eyes. An inch from her ear, he whispered, "Do you want to live, laddie?"

Tom stepped forward as if to come to her aid but Christopher stopped him with a growl, "Stay back, this doesn't concern you." And Tom stayed back.

Christopher returned his attention to the immobilized Katherine and pressed the tip of the blade against her throat. "Now laddie, I asked you a question."

"Yes," whispered Katherine back, barely able to breathe,

but fully aware her life depended on her answer. And fully aware of the necklace hidden under her bulky clothing. If he should discover it . . . .

"What was that again?"

"Yes!" she said more clearly, praying for him to let go.

Satisfied, he released her. Katherine, trembling and coughing, clung to the wheel to steady herself as Christopher casually strolled away from her and sheathed the knife.

"Now, keeping the fact that you want to live in mind, tell me why I should let you live. Tell me how you can be of use to me. I see you can handle a wheel but there's many aboard who can do that. And I've seen you help the dwarf cook but we need only one cook. And you're as weak and soft-skinned as a newborn babe, so you're of no use to me as a fighter. So what use are you to me?"

Katherine frantically ran over all the subjects she had mastered in her education, desperate to dredge up some knowledge, some talent she might have which would interest him enough to leave her alone. "I can translate for you," she offered up first.

"No good. I've got Dutchmen, Frenchmen, Portuguese, Swedes and plenty others aboard who know enough to rob in twenty languages. What else?"

Katherine tried again. "I can write, keep records. I'm skillful with pen and paper."

"You mean you can keep records so that if we get captured, the judges will have more evidence to hang us by? Do you think I'm crack-brained!? What else?"

"I know mathematics, I could figure your accounts for you."

Finally he seemed interested and he stopped scowling. "Now, that I might be able to use. When we take a rich prize we'll want to make sure it's all divvied up proper. What else?"

What else could she say of her expensive and privileged upbringing which was so valuable in the milieu in which she came from . . . but which was so useless here? That she rode well? That she could recite vast portions of the *Aeneid* in Latin or the *Odyssey* in Greek? That she could skillfully copy a Leonardo drawing? That she could distinguish fine wines and cheeses? That she could design and embroider complicated tapestries full of unicorns and phoenixes?

Maybe that was something.

"Well?" Christopher demanded impatiently.

"Sew," she said.

"So?"

"Sew, sewing," she explained.

"You mean tailoring?"

"Yes, of course." Now was not the time to quibble over terms.

"Since when do priests learn tailoring?"

"I am not a priest." She was tired of explaining that. "I am just a student. Students must learn all sorts of things."

"Well, padre," he said with a trace of amusement, "you just saved your skin. We can use a tailor. Those on shore charge us four times what they charge the landlubbers and only do half as good a job for us at that. Just look at this!"

He came up close to her again to point out the ripped lace on what had once been a fine plum-colored velvet coat but which was now stained and faded and torn.

"Yes," he agreed, locking his eyes deliberately with hers. "Yes, we can use you if you're what you say you are. You can show us a sample of your work tomorrow. And then we'll take a vote to see if it passes muster.

"And, laddie," he added, "you'd better not be lying to me about this. We cut out liars' tongues, you know."

XIII
NEEDLE AND THREAD

The next day Katherine signed the *Articles* and passed muster as a tailor simply by reattaching a sleeve to a shirt without any knots. Being totally ignorant of fine details, the crew pronounced her work excellent.

In truth, of course, the only sewing Katherine had done was delicate embroidery using golden needles and silken threads. Her mother's dressmakers took care of all the mundane needlework. Katherine never had any reason to learn how clothes were put together, or how to repair a seam or alter a shoulder or patch a pocket. But, using a combination of analysis, conjecture and invention, she figured it out.

A surprising number of the crew, filthy low-life scum though they were to her, fancied themselves dandies. Consequently her new skill brought her instant appreciation . . . and a protection of sorts.

Out came all the finery stolen from a half dozen ships — velvet waistcoats, embroidered vests, satin knee breeches, linen shirts with ruffled lace cuffs, and brocade longcoats with braid and brass buttons. As soon as she finished altering or repairing them the owners snatched them back, chucked their old garb into the sea, and donned their fancy new togs.

However, after a few weeks of constant wear, the bright colors darkened, the shiny brass buttons dulled and the fragile lace cuffs disintegrated. Their finery was fine no longer.

So out came more stolen booty which kept Katherine busy throughout the entire daylight hours. But she didn't object to the constant pile before her at all for it not only helped pass the hours, it ensured her preservation. No one else could do what she could, therefore no one dared bother her.

Katherine had appropriated a small wedge of the fore-castle up by the bow, claiming she needed the light. In truth, she stayed on deck because she found the stench belowdecks from the rotting refuse in the bottom of the hull almost un-bearable. No matter what the weather she only went below decks for a few hours at night after almost everyone else was asleep. She slept in the hold with the others, packed side by side on the floor with them like dogs. Because she never re-moved her own cloak nor her protective layers of clothing, she soon began to feel as grimy and disheveled as every one else looked.

And so her days and nights passed. After a few weeks Katherine could understand why the *Articles* were necessary. Most of the non-navigating men spent their days in a state of absolute boredom. Once their weapons were in top condi-tion, once their steel was polished and the ship's hand gre-nades created out of empty wine bottles, shot and powder, there was nothing for them to do but grouse, drink, and play cards or dice. At such close quarters due to the overcrowding, tempers flared frequently.

Once Katherine began to be able to distinguish one cut-throat from another, she observed that the men sometimes gave evidence of less than total commitment to their alliance. After all, they were not a homogeneous unit who had sailed and fought together for years. For some it was their first voyage on the *Taingire*, for others their fourth. Katherine had counted nine distinct nationalities on board — each of which tended to be suspicious of each of the others. Brian Christo-pher, the captain, was from Ireland. Bucko, the vicious former quartermaster, had been born in the West Indies. The boatswain, called Le Grand because of the bulge in his breeches, was French. The crippled former cook, Smutje, was Dutch. Ben the Bosun was from the American colonies and Hawkins who set the sails was British. Britain seemed to account for the greatest number.

Tom told her why. "Every town and village in England has a quota to fill. Rather than risk losing their favorite sons when the government press gangs come 'round, the mayors use the occasion to clean out their jails. These "Newgate Birds" or "King's Hard Bargains" wind up, often as not, jumping ship at the first foreign port and quickly reverting to their criminal ways. Both at sea and on land, now."

"So these men are all convicts?" asked Katherine.

"No, some are legitimate sailors, or fishermen, or farmers or whoever maybe hit a spell of bad luck."

"Like you?"

"Like me," he acknowledged.

The only European country that did not seem to be represented was Spain. Katherine thought this might be because Spain was the principal quarry of the pirate group. All aboard the *Taingire* dreamed of a great Spanish prize, of a great Spanish galleon overflowing with gold and silver. That was the only dream they all shared: the Prize.

In actuality the crew cared nothing deep down for the *Taingire*, sailing, Christopher, religion, politics, or each other. In greed for "the Prize" alone were they united. That's why the *Articles* and all the other rules were so necessary. The rigidity of the rules kept this disparate group in line for the common good.

Katherine found out just how strictly the *Articles'* edicts were enforced after only a week aboard.

A short broad fellow named Paddy, while smoking a pipe one morning, went down to the hold to retrieve something, his pipe still in his mouth. Fire being the terror of seamen, no smoking or open flame was ever allowed belowdecks under any circumstances. For this reason water tubs were set handy all around, even on the upper decks, should sparks fly. More than likely, Paddy merely forgot the pipe was in his mouth and his transgression was therefore unintentional. But his violation of the prohibition was noticed and he had to stand trial.

"Forty lashes," decreed the jurymen.

After Bucko volunteered to administer the punishment, the unfortunate Paddy was lashed to the capstan and given an iron musket ball to hold between his teeth so he could not bite his tongue in two. Then Bucko took out his cat-o'-nine-tails and began. Slowly and methodically he swung the vicious whip as a hundred men watched and counted out each stroke aloud. "Sixteen, seventeen, eighteen" — at this point the skin had broken and rivulets of blood appeared — "twenty-seven, twenty-eight, twenty-nine" — the blood flowed so profusely that it spattered to the deck at each lash — "thirty-eight, thirty-nine, forty!"

Finally the spectacle ended and the ashen-faced Paddy was untied. He immediately sank to his knees as one kindly fellow blotted his back and another brought him a double measure of rum. He grasped the ladle with trembling hands, spit out the musket ball, and then drank the rum down without pause. When he finished some of the men cheered him, for he had endured his punishment and not cried out. In appreciation for the cheers he smiled weakly and let two of the men half-drag, half-carry him down belowdecks to get his wounds treated by Matto.

Later that day Katherine saw the musket ball rolling around on the deck. It had been flattened and indented with teeth marks.

* * * * *

Day after tedious day passed as the *Taingire* leisurely moved west with the trade winds. They had not spied ship nor land for over a month and provisions were again running low. Each day men waited for that cry from the crow's nest that meant everything to them: "A sail! A sail!" The first man who spotted a sail was promised his pick of the best small arm aboard her. Unless the sail was that from a British naval ship.

And so they waited for the cry that could mean death . . . or could mean a Spanish treasure galleon full of gold and silver from Mexico, or a Portuguese merchantman with gold and jewels from Brazil in her hold, or an East Indiaman off her course, or a slaver full of ivory and men to sell at huge profit.

Day after day men climbed high upon the yard to search the horizon. Once, when the mast was damp and slippery, a young fellow lost his foothold and fell overboard. Men rushed to the rail but there was no way to turn back. So they shrugged and the boy was lost. For several days after, the crew climbed far more carefully aloft.

But still no sail.

As the *Taingire* neared the tropics the weather warmed. Men discarded the heavy coats and capes they had fought over the previous month and now strolled about barefoot, in sunburns and open shirts. At last Katherine, too, reluctantly removed her cloak, but she kept on her cap and two shirts and a vest to flatten her small breasts. She also kept the neck tabs on her shirts tightly fastened and covered by a silky cravat wrapped several times around her neck to hide any suspicious lumps from the ruby necklace under her shirt. When some of the men heckled her for not opening her shirt, she replied that she did not wish to risk a painful burn.

"If you've such tender skin," they chided her, " 'tis a good thing we're not cannibals. If we were, we'd eat you first." Then they laughed. But by now they did not scare her so much so she pretended to laugh with them and they left her alone.

In truth Katherine's skin was tender and remarkably unmarked compared with everyone else's aboard. Although most were youthful, at least half of the company showed evidence on their bodies of dread diseases. And the warmer it got and the worse their diets got, the sicker they got. Matto had already diagnosed cases of dysentery, scurvy, touches of malaria and yellow fever and, most of all, venereal disease. So prevalent was the latter affliction that the store of mercurial compounds from the *Mag Mell*'s stolen medicine chest had been used up within the first week. Within three weeks all that remained in the chest was a little gin for use with potato juice as a remedy for poison fish.

Conditions aboard the *Taingire* got worse and worse. There were no feasts now, no casual gorging on chickens in claret. The chickens had run out. The claret had run out. Almost everything had run out. Men smoked all day long to ease their growling stomachs until the tobacco ran out, too. A green scum had developed on what remained of the drinking water. The teeth of the older men started loosening. Eyes started glazing over above sunken cheekbones. A lethargy took hold of the weakest of them.

And still no cry of "A sail! A sail!" to save them. Or end their misery.

Finally, those that were still able to muster the energy stepped over their prostrate cohorts and gathered on deck to take a vote. They voted overwhelmingly to divide up what they had and make for land and fresh provisions. Then, they feebly joked, after a few weeks on shore with "one of those handsome black-eyed mulatter plantation gals," they'd be ready to set sail for "the Prize" once again.

Hope stirred in Katherine for the first time in weeks. Land! That word now promised escape as certain as the word "sea" once promised escape in Padua. *Land!* On land her nightmare would be over. A port city had to have a government, a council that would aid and protect her when she told them her story. Maybe they could even get her stolen gold and jewels back for her. She would state her case before the city elders and see justice done at last.

I'll bloody well see them all hang, she thought.

XIV
THE GREAT DESIRE

Toward dusk, three days after the vote, a dark speck appeared on the horizon. The thrilling cry of "Land ho!" rang out from the crow's nest.

Saved! thought the crew of the *Taingire*. Saved from death by starvation.

Saved! thought Katherine. Saved from death by the crew of the *Taingire*.

Rather than risk an unnecessary hazard, that of attempting a landing in the dark, Christopher ordered the crew to take in all sail but the main and slowed the *Taingire* down. They would land on the Bahamian island in the morning.

That night more than her empty stomach kept Katherine awake. In the fever of excitement she paced the deck, breathing in the soft tropical air. She imagined she smelled fruit and palms and flowers; she imagined she smelled food cooking; she imagined she smelled hope and sanctuary. She hadn't felt so alive with restless anticipating since that last night in Padua. Then, too, she had eagerly awaited the morning light, certain it would bring precious freedom. It hadn't. But surely this next dawn would.

But the next morning, from the harbor of New Providence, Katherine's hopes were crushed once more. In bitter disappointment she stood at the rail and stared at the arena before her. The pirates' harbor of New Providence was as far from the civilized town of her imaginings as her present status of barefoot servant was from her past status of spoiled grande dame.

In a settlement of over two thousand she saw only three crude buildings made of wood — two taverns and a store-house. All the other businesses and dwellings looked to be merely lean-tos made of driftwood and sail, or tents draped over broken spars — with no order to them and no thought of permanence.

As soon as the *Taingire* anchored, men rushed to the long-boat, pushing and shoving each other to be in the first group ashore. The stronger and healthier ones won, the weaker and sicker had to wait. In their lust for the provisions and plea-sures of the port, no one paid the slightest attention to Kath-erine. So along about the sixth shuttle she was able to slip in amongst others and row with them to shore.

Despite her disappointment, when she finally felt solid land beneath her feet, she gave thanks. True, the land was white sand littered and stinking with refuse from the seamy shanty town, but it did offer safety and space and privacy and food. Food! That's what Katherine's protruding bones and growling stomach demanded. Food to give her strength.

She had a few coins in her pocket, coins she had been given as tips when she had particularly pleased some of the cutthroats with her needlework. So she stepped up to a large negro, naked to the waist, and pointed to some mangoes he had in a basket. With a smile, he gave her three for her coin and split them open for her while speaking in a tongue unrec-ognizable to Katherine.

She fell to the sand right there and started sucking up the sweet, sticky meat of the fruit, oblivious to everything but filling her stomach.

"You'd better eat that slower, laddie," came a voice from above her. She looked up and saw Christopher holding a glass and grinning at her. "You eat too fast on an empty stomach, it'll all come right back up." Then, having given her all the attention he was going to, he turned his back and walked away to have his glass refilled.

Picking up the rest of her meal, Katherine quickly hurried out of his sight. As the mangoes began to take effect Katherine began to feel better and used her renewed energy to walk about. She passed men of every color in the open air — fighting, boozing, gambling, smoking, conspiring, cursing or snoring. Although it was only mid-morning, Katherine saw the bodies of already besotted residents lying about the white sand beach, too drunk or lazy to brush off the swarms of flies that circled them and the half-eaten fruit which lay rotting by their campsites. Katherine spotted only a few white women — most of the females were black or mulatto. Scores of naked half-caste children ran about as their mothers roasted turtles, pigs and goats over open flames.

So this, Katherine thought, is the great refuge for pirates, whores, criminals, mutineers, jobless laborers, traders, and runaway slaves, servants and soldiers. Not one man she passed looked respectable, not one looked trustworthy, not one looked as if he could be of any help to her at all.

This great refuge was no refuge for Katherine.

After buying some roasted pork from one of the women surrounded by naked children, Katherine began to walk faster. Past the dogs sniffing refuse, past the tattered lean-tos, past the bodies on the beaches, past even the beaches themselves. She walked all the way up the high coral hills that ringed the harbor.

From that viewpoint she could behold all the destruction the pirates had wrought to what once must have been a paradise. In the beautiful blue snug harbor lay dozens of gutted hulls of derelict and abandoned vessels. Because of the safety of its shallow depth — large man-of-war ships couldn't enter it — the harbor was choked with sloops, brigantines, and tenders. Even from the distance the settlement seemed squalid and fetid.

So Katherine turned her back to the harbor and to the mangy men who had contaminated it. She had spotted a spring and she followed it inland. And at last she found a sort of refuge.

The fresh-water spring led upstream into a lush tropical forest where giant tree ferns blocked out the sun. With each step she took into the shadows of this eerie wilderness, all sounds and smells of man disappeared. Brilliantly colored parrots squawked to her from the crotches of mangrove trees. Tiny tree frogs sang to her from the canopy of foliage above her head. Fuchsia, violet and pink orchids bloomed at her feet along with masses of other species of flower for which Katherine had no name. Exotic thick vines tripped her when her attention was diverted to some new wonder.

In the dim bluish light a deep peace sank into her body and bones and she stretched out on the soft moss by the stream and rested. Katherine felt like a modern Odysseus, alone in a strange and enchanted isle on which, she thought with a smile, nymphs and fauns, gnomes and trolls, ogres and jinns might very well live behind each tree.

And, as if in response to her imaginings, one popped out.

Totally taken by surprise, she screamed and a flock of yellow-bellied bananaquits immediately flew off above her with an alarming screech.

Matto.

It was Matto who had dropped like a bolt out of the blue upon her.

"Ah, Mistress," he said, breathing heavily. "I thought you would never stop climbing. My legs are not as long as yours you know." And he too sank down on the mossy rug.

"I am not your mistress any longer, Matto," said Katherine coldly. It was the first she had spoken to him in six weeks.

"Master, then," responded the undaunted and unoffended Matto.

"Nor your master. That all changed forever the second we set foot on the *Taingire*."

"Why do you blame me for that?"

"And whom else should I blame? Had you not opened your mouth when we were attacked, I should have stayed on the *Mag Mell* and ultimately been rescued. And safe."

"Ah, Mistress, have you not learned anything? Are you still so blind? I saved your life by my quick action. You should thank me, not reproach me!"

Katherine looked at him with scorn.

"The *Mag Mell* was a doomed ship," he continued. "Without sails, she would only drift with the winds and the currents. Without provisions, her crew would slowly starve. And without a well-caulked bottom, she would surely sink when the worms had their fill."

Katherine lay silent, her hands behind her head, not responding. But she listened.

"I see you still don't believe me," he continued. "All right then, say you remained aboard the *Mag Mell* and the improbable did occur and you were rescued before you starved to death or drowned. What then? The pirates had stolen all your gold. You have never been penniless, Mistress. I doubt you could survive that. Or wish to survive that. For there's only one way for a poor woman to make money. And that's the way of those women you looked at with such disgust down there on the beach. Oh no, that way is not for a high-born lady of Padua!"

Matto was mocking her and Katherine knew it.

"You forget, Matto, that I was not penniless. I still had my wedding necklace." She felt her throat to comfort herself.

He noticed the gesture. "I thought as much. And I," he said, reaching in his pocket, "still have a few gold crowns." He showed them to her.

"I don't think they'll do us much good here."

"No," agreed Matto, "they would only attract attention. And we don't want to attract any more attention."

Lying in the soft, sweet-smelling moss, far away from the cursed ships and the cursed crews of the harbor, Katherine softened in her attitude toward Matto. Maybe she had judged him wrongly. Maybe he was thinking of her own good when he had connived her transfer from the *Mag Mell* to the *Taingire*. Maybe he was on her side after all.

Of course he was, she finally concluded, or he would have betrayed her great secret. He did what he thought was best for both of them. As he had promised.

And so Katherine forgave him as Matto knew she would. Christopher had been correct that day aboard the *Mag Mell* when he said that servants knew their masters ten times better than masters knew their servants.

"So what do we do now?" Katherine asked, plucking a brilliant pink blossom from the crevice of a rock and breathing in its strong sweet odor.

"Well first, if I were you, I'd bury that necklace in a safe place. The days are getting longer and hotter and you soon won't be able to stand having that scarf tied so tightly around your neck."

What he said made sense for she already sweated under the many layers. By removing the scarf at least she could open the top of her shirts to cool off a little while still keeping her vest tightly buttoned. And so she finally unwound the silky cravat, damp with her sweat, then unlatched the necklace and rolled it up in the cloth. Matto in the meantime had found a narrow stone and had started scraping away the soft moss from the side of a large palm tree. He watched as Katherine dropped the small bundle into the shallow hole. Then both she and Matto covered it with rich, moist black soil. When they patted it down and spread scraps of green fungus over, no one could tell anything had been disturbed.

Katherine felt relieved now that the great weight had been lifted from her neck.

"Now what?"

"Now," he said with enthusiasm, "we make plans."

"We could steal a tender, or a longboat, or even a small sloop one night," Katherine suggested. "There must be 400 ships in the harbor to choose from."

"And go where? Have you seen any charts? Do you know where we are on the map? And supposing we make it out of the harbor without being spotted, which way would we sail?"

"Before the wind, of course."

"And what if the wind happens to be blowing back to New Providence? Or to be blowing out to the great sea from whence we came? Or not to be blowing at all? Anyone can sail with a good wind but have you learned how to sail with a bad one?"

"No," Katherine confessed. Her education in navigation had ceased the day the *Mag Mell* met the *Taingire*.

But a solution came to her. "Perhaps we could convince Tom Tyrell to join us. He has the skill. And he's not really a pirate."

"Oh no?" questioned Matto. "Well, he's certainly acting like one. I heard him demanding a share of the booty off the *Mag Mell* when they divided it up yesterday afternoon. I'm sure he plans to ship out with them again."

"Oh," said Katherine, disappointed. She had not known that.

The two lapsed into silence, each running over possibilities in their heads, rejecting them, and thinking up more.

"What if," offered Katherine, "we bribe one of the traders who's running legitimate merchandise to the colonies to take us on? Or, better yet, we could sign aboard her, you as cook again and me as an ordinary seaman. Then we wouldn't have to show any of our gold."

Katherine watched as Matto considered her suggestion.

"Yes," he finally said, shaking his head slowly and looking at her shrewdly. "Yes, you certainly look more like a sailor than a lady now. It might very well work. That is," he quickly added, "if there indeed is a legitimate merchantman to be found midst this pack of thieves. I'll ask around. If there is one to be found, I'll find him," he boasted.

That settled, the old impish smile of the Matto she knew from her childhood returned to his face. "Not that this is such a bad place, Mistress," he said, settling back and gesturing around them. "A mild climate, fruit for the plucking, lobsters, turtles, fish, wild goats and pigs, all free. Some would consider this paradise."

"You'll find those who do," she retorted, "rotting brainless and besotted down there on the beach."

"Even the Garden of Eden had its snake," he teased.

"Well, this Garden of Eden has at least two thousand of them. The sooner we get away, the less likely we are to be bitten."

XV
MAD AND MERRY

Matto and Katherine built their own lean-to up on the coral hill. From there they could keep track of the comings and goings of all the ships in the harbor but still escape the noise and smell and rabble of the settlement.

Once they had a shelter of sorts from the sun, their lives fell into a steady routine. Matto spent most of his days idling with the populace, gathering information and earning small tips for his tricks. Katherine spent most of her days alone, trekking through the woods and coves, gathering food, and enjoying her blossoming physical strength and autonomy.

And so their days passed until one bright April afternoon when Matto returned to their hilltop shelter all excited. "I found us a ship!" he announced with a flourish. "There's a trader in town, a Frenchman named La Breton, just in from Guadeloupe, who'll sign us on. He's got a cargo of French silks and laces for the good citizens of Charleston. England, it seems, has forbidden the Americans from trading with anyone but the English. So non-English goods bring premium prices. La Breton stands to make a fortune."

"But if such trade is against English law," asked Katherine, "won't it be dangerous for us?" She had finally learned to think of the practical things first.

"La Breton claims that no one has ever stopped him. Indeed, to the contrary, he is welcomed in the finest homes in America. The colonists want the trade. It's only England who doesn't want it. And England is three thousand miles away."

He paused, then added, "Most of the time."

Standing on the hill overlooking the sea, Katherine thought over the offer. "Which ship is the Frenchman's?" she asked.

Matto pointed to a sleek three-masted barkentine.

"She looks sturdy enough."

"She's made the voyage many times, Mistress."

"When does she sail?"

"Within the week. La Breton is buying up all the stolen luxury goods in port, offering gold and munitions for them. The Americans, he says, are so desperate for his goods that they never ask where he got them.

"This is our chance, Mistress, if you ever want to leave this island."

Yes, thought Katherine, *maybe this is our chance. Our chance to return to a semblance of civilization where law and order, learning and manners still counted for something.*

"All right, Matto," she decided, "tell Monsieur La Breton he has two new hands."

"You'll have to see him yourself. He insists on checking out all the men who sail under him. Seems he's deathly afraid of disease and wants to make sure you have no fever."

"Where do I find him?"

"At the rum shop by the storehouse tonight."

Katherine nodded. "All right then, I'll go."

She waited for the sun to set before starting her descent to the den of thieves below. She dressed as plainly as possible in order to draw the least amount of attention to herself from the endless groups of riffraff shouting and swearing, drinking and gambling, fighting and whoring. She stepped over bodies lying both prone and supine in the sand, ducked to avoid being hit by flying bottles, and swerved to avoid coming face to face with anyone.

Finally she reached Liverpool Annie's Rum Shop. But when she entered, she could make out very little at first. Heavy smoke hung in the fetid air. That, combined with the insufficient lamplight, succeeded in obscuring the features of most present. A ferocious din of laughter and singing, shouting and bombast, assaulted her ears. Serving women in bare feet and tattered gowns passed by carrying heavy pewter plates of stew and mugs of rum. One blonde one winked at Katherine as she brushed by her.

Proceeding slowly until her eyes adjusted, Katherine finally spotted the well-fed figure of a man she assumed, from his dress, to be La Breton. The man, who wore a three-cornered hat and silk stockings, stood out blatantly in his fastidious attire. A ledger lay by his right hand and in his left hand he held a lace handkerchief from which he periodically inhaled some essence of perfume to protect him from the befouled air.

As Katherine approached his table he was in the process of concluding a dealing with a one-eyed cripple, paying the fellow five gold crowns for a diamond and amethyst brooch which Katherine, having learned to judge the value of jewels from her mother, knew to be worth twenty times that. But the cripple did not object, he just grinned toothlessly and pocketed the coin, no doubt to gamble and drink it away that very night.

"That brooch is worth a hundred crowns at least," she said in French over the hubbub to announce her presence.

La Breton looked up from the ledger in which he was recording the sale and appraised her with as little emotion as he had appraised the brooch. "I expect to get two hundred in the colonies." He responded in French and gestured for her to sit. Her person was apparently not as offensive to him as the cripple's for he stopped breathing through his kerchief. Indeed, thanks to rinsing out her laundry and bathing regularly in the interior streams of the island, Katherine was most likely the cleanest person on it.

"And what have you come to peddle?" he asked her as she brushed aside the offer of a glass of rum from the serving maid.

"Nothing," she replied in the same business-like tone, "but myself. I hear you have a ship bound for Charleston. I've come to sign aboard her."

"You are a sailor?"

She nodded.

"A sailor who refuses a glass of rum?" He cocked one eyebrow at her. "You will pardon me for being suspicious, but I have never heard of a sailor who ever refused a drop. Now, spies, I have known spies who did not touch it. You would not be a spy, now would you? Sent from the English?"

Katherine shook her head.

"Ah, I know! You are the one the dwarf spoke of, correct? You are, how shall I put it, companions?"

"That is as good a way to put it as any," she replied. Katherine saw no reason to explain her relationship with Matto. She saw no reason to explain anything now. Let the Frenchman think whatever he pleased.

"All right then. You're a little young for me but I can always use a sober hand. Sign here and with good wind you'll be in Charleston within two weeks." He handed her his pen and a long sheet of paper which was already half filled with mostly illegible names and X's. With a flourish Katherine signed her brother's name and silently handed back the paper and pen.

"I'll raise a signal flag the day before we sail. Watch for it."

"I will," she promised and started to rise to leave. But just then a heavy hand clamped down on her shoulder and forced her to sit back down.

"Well, if it isn't my dago priest!"

Katherine looked up into the grinning mien of Brian Christopher. He kept his left hand tightly on her shoulder, drained a glass of rum with his right, and continued the unwelcome conversation. "I'd wondered where you ran off to. I've seen the little fellow around but you, you just disappeared. Of course knowing how high above us all you are I figured maybe you ran into someone who took offense at the way you looked at him, and got yourself killed.

"But now here you are," he said, gesturing with his empty glass to La Breton, "signing up to go to sea with this scoundrel who's a greater thief in his own way than I am in mine."

"This one of your men, Christopher?" asked La Breton, switching easily to English.

"No," answered Katherine in English with a boldness born of the fact that she carried her own knife and pistol now and had learned to use them well in the weeks of daily hunting. She was not the same helpless and hopeless shorn lamb she had been aboard the *Taingire*. She was not so afraid of him anymore. Nor of anyone anymore.

But Christopher disagreed with her answer. "Yes," he told La Breton, "he's mine and now I'm claiming him."

With that settled, he dragged Katherine up from her seat and over to a chair at his table in the corner. From years of hauling sails and anchors, his arms were strong as steel and just as unyielding. Pushing her into a corner chair, he sat down opposite her and announced, "You owe me a song, padre." Then, from a strolling musician he grabbed a battered instrument and shoved it at her. "Now here's a lute for you, so play! I like to dine with music in my ears."

And then he ignored her and settled down to his stew and called for another glass of rum.

Katherine examined the once-fine piece in her hands.

Months of ill-treatment had left scratches and dirt and dents on its surface which marred its original exquisite lines. But to Katherine's amazement all the strings were intact. Apparently the lute had not been played much since its theft, just carried around and knocked around and bartered around.

Katherine considered her situation. As Christopher sat between her and the exit she prudently decided to pacify him and play. From the volume of liquor that was disappearing down his throat, Katherine knew that it was only a matter of time before he passed out.

She could wait. She'd become an expert at it since she'd met him.

"I know no jigs or sailors' songs," she told him truthfully.

"Play what you know, then," he said without looking up from his bowl.

So she took the lute and tuned the strings and thought of the last time she had played. It was at one of her father's receptions at the villa. With her father on the cello and Emogena on the harp and herself on the lute and harpsichord, they had played Vivaldi, Scarlatti, and Telemann. But now she had no father, no sister, no villa, and no sedate patrician audience. Now she had a smoke-filled room on a tiny island filled with the dregs of the earth who would just as soon slit her throat as look at her.

But she played, hesitantly and awkwardly at first, then more confidently as her fingers remembered the familiar notes. She played a fugue of Corelli, a sonata of Bassani, then several melancholy sarabandes. She blocked out the chaos around her and played as if she were alone. She let herself enter the music and let the music carry her away. And when she finished and looked up Christopher was staring at her so intently and so truly that she pulled back, and felt suddenly self-conscious and wary.

But the terrible light was gone from his eyes and his shoulders sagged as if he were greatly fatigued. "I'm impressed, padre," he said quietly and without sarcasm. It was the first time she had heard him speak that way. And look that way. "You know any songs with words?" he asked.

"Only in Italian or French," she said, almost truthfully for the only English lyrics she had learned from the company she had been keeping were along the lines of "I was just a goddam fool in the port o' Liverpool" and "I'll drink it hot, I'll drink it cold, I'll drink it new, I'll drink it old."

"Then I'll teach you some," he announced, returning to his usual domineering manner. "The Irish are great singers you know. See if you can follow me." And he sang:

> Come live with me and be my love,
> And we will all the pleasures prove
> That hills and valleys, dales and fields,
> And all the craggy mountains yields.
>
> And we will sit upon the rocks
> Seeing the shepherds feed their flocks,
> By shallow rivers, to whose falls
> Melodious birds sing madrigals.

He had such a fine strong voice that several tables around them ceased their chatter to listen. But as soon as the last note faded, the clatter and chatter resumed. Christopher, mellowed by the drink and music, smiled at Katherine for the first time. And when the maid came by with another glass for him, he grabbed the woman's hips and recited: "All are keen, to know who'll sleep with blonde Doreen; all Doreen herself will own, is that she will not sleep alone." Doreen, if that indeed was her name, merely laughed and pulled away.

Christopher turned his attention back to Katherine. The liquor kept his tongue loose.

"Be ye from a sunny land, laddie?"

Katherine nodded.

"Not I. I'm from the northern tip of Ireland where the icy blasts come down from Greenland even in the summer. Where the cold and drizzle numbs your joints and the ice makes your hands bleed. Everything is grey up there, the fog, the sky, the sea, the stone, the mist, the people. I was never warm a full day in my life until I left.

"I left of my own free will to join Her Majesty's Royal Navy when I was thirteen, a beardless lad like you. Younger than you. Up there I had no chance of a tomorrow that was anything but a repeat of a yesterday. I wanted a different tomorrow."

"You certainly got it," Katherine commented dryly.

"Ay, that I did. But I also wanted to be rich as well. And that I haven't got yet. Yet."

He paused, reminiscing. "You know it's been more than twenty years since I left Ireland but there's not a day goes by that I don't thank God that I'm not freezing in that cold grey wind. Even when I was kidnapped later in Bristol and shipped out as an indentured servant to labour on a Barbados plantation, I even thanked God then. At least I was warm. At least I felt the sun on my back. As well as my master's whip."

"So why did you leave Barbados?"

"According to the paper I had been forced to sign I was supposed to be able to buy my freedom after five years of servitude. But the devil of a master kept extending the debt until I was nothing more than a bloody slave.

"So I ran away and snuck on board the first ship that anchored. She was a privateer. But what did I care? The fellows were jolly and I had coins jingling in my pocket for the first time."

"Stolen coins," said Katherine.

"And have you, your Lordship," Christopher corrosively responded, "never stolen?"

"Never," claimed Katherine, conveniently forgetting her behavior on her wedding day.

"But your father's a rich man is he not? One of the landed gentry?"

"You could call it that, I suppose."

"And how did he get to be a rich man? How did he make all this money?"

"I don't know." Katherine suddenly realized that she really didn't know where her father's money came from. He traded a little and talked about the "estates" a little. And her mother brought a fine dowry with her. But that's all she knew about it. Katherine, born to wealth and privilege, had always taken it for granted. Until recently, of course.

"Well, I'll tell you how your father gets his money. Like all the other gentry, by robbing the poor. Now I," Christopher said almost smugly, "I rob only the rich. And I'll tell you why. I'll tell you because you're a smart lad. A pain in the ass, but a smart one. And you'll understand."

Christopher paused, then leaned forward as if sharing a confidence. "Now a man can be hanged for stealing a shilling, is it not so?"

Katherine nodded.

"So stealing a fortune makes much more sense, doesn't it?" By his tone Katherine could tell he found his own logic irrefutable.

"But why steal at all?" she asked.

"What else is a man to do? I've no rich parents nor fancy education like you."

Katherine, well-skilled in the art of polemics, could not contain her tongue. "So you see your way of life as a means to compensate for the injustices you have suffered?"

"No," he grinned, "I see my way of life as a means to make vast sums of money."

"And that is why you became a pirate captain?"

"Well, I figured if I was going to be a pirate and risk the rope, I'd bloody well better be captain. I like being my own master and I especially like the double share. Some day when I capture a big enough prize I'll buy myself a sugar plantation. Ah, laddie, that's truly the life. Lying in the sun all day, while others do all the work for you." He smiled, "Yes, with a fine woman by my side I'll live out my days on some golden island and never be poor or cold again."

And, with eyes closed, he sang:

> And I will make thee beds of roses
> And a thousand fragrant posies,
> A cap of flowers, and a kirtle
> Embroidered all with leaves of myrtle;
>
> A gown made of the finest wool,
> Which from our pretty lambs we pull;
> Fair lined slippers for the cold,
> With buckles of the purest gold;
>
> A belt of straw and ivy buds
> With coral clasps and amber studs;
> And if these pleasures may thee move,
> Come live with me and be my love.
>
> The shepherd swains shall dance and sing
> For thy delight each May morning:
> If these delights thy mind may move,
> Then live with me and be my love.

XVI
THESE KNAVES

Katherine spent the next few days back in the comparative safety of her hilltop hideaway, watching the activity in the harbor and waiting for La Breton's signal flag.

Christopher had ordered the *Taingire* beached and careened. From the heights, Katherine could easily keep track of the progress. She watched as Tom Tyrell supervised the job. First he ordered the ship unloaded, then hauled over on its side to expose her bottom. Then came the tedious job of scraping off the seaweed and barnacles and examining the wood under for teredo worms. When any were found, the planks were replaced. Once the *Taingire*'s hull was sufficiently cleaned, her seams were recaulked and a concoction of pitch, tar, sulphur and arsenic was applied in a thick coat.

Of course the *Taingire* wasn't the only vessel being careened in New Providence's harbor. All warm water vessels had to be careened at least three times a year and New Providence was just about the best place to do it. For once a pirate's ship was beached and on her side, there would be no means of escape for her crew should they be discovered. In New Providence, the cutthroats could careen their ships at leisure. Here they were safe.

In fact, they were so safe that many vowed to never leave: "Give me a knife to hunt food, a couple yards of calico to cover my body, a palm fond to protect my head from the sun, a dark gal to share my hammock in the long summer night, and a bottomless keg of rum, and I'll never stray," many said.

But stray they did. When their money was drunk and gambled away or when rumors came that a rich merchantman would be sailing soon out of Portobello or Charleston or Suriname, suddenly a hammock and a few yards of calico weren't enough. Nothing was enough but chest after chest of gold.

That's why, when the rumor swept the island that the Spanish fleet was about to sail, men's eyes glittered. From reprobate to reprobate, from tavern to tavern, from shanty to shanty, the story spread. One ship was said to contain a hundred chests of diamonds, another thousands of pounds of gold bullion, another tens of thousands of silver ingots, another millions of pieces of eight.

With each telling the quantities multiplied and men's eyes misted over with the unholy vision of endless wealth. With each tide, more ships disappeared from the harbor. Every man still able to swing a cutlass clamored to sign aboard any ship with sails.

Except La Breton's. He considered himself a legitimate trader. Consequently, he wanted no part of such hot-blooded rashness with all its potential dangers and all its probable fruitlessness. Nevertheless, even he was affected by the frenzy of activity for most of the crew he had earlier signed had deserted under the promise of "the Prize." La Breton was forced to delay his sailing.

As the population dwindled, Katherine took to meeting each afternoon with him to check on his progress. He welcomed her for he found her one of the few persons on the island whose company he could tolerate. He also enjoyed chess and found in Katherine a willing partner. As they sat in the shade of a palm within view of the few ships still in the harbor — one being his and another the *Taingire* — he explained why the delay did not bother him.

"If they capture no prize they'll soon come forlornly back

and I'll be able to muster a crew at even lower wages. And if they do capture a prize, they'll still have to come back to trade the miscellaneous booty through me. So you see, either way I stand to gain. Everything comes to he who waits," he pontificated as he took Katherine's knight with his rook and put her in check.

"Only old age comes to he who waits," answered Katherine as she took his rook with her queen and checkmated him.

"Well said," commented an all-too-familiar voice. Christopher, accompanied by Tom, strode up to their makeshift table and joined their conversation uninvited. "Better a short and merry life than a long and woeful one. No prey, no pay, hey, padre?" he joked to Katherine.

To La Breton he said, "You'd better take it easy. I've seen men your size keel over and die on a hot day like this."

La Breton was not amused. "Christopher," he snapped, "why aren't you out there with the rest of your kind?"

"I fully intend to be. Tonight. The *Taingire* sails with the tide tonight."

"I've heard the fleet is well-armed and well-escorted this year. And no one knows what course they will take. Even if you should perchance stumble on them, you'll be in no shape to challenge a whole fleet all by yourself. You'll be blown out of the water." La Breton smiled to show just how unconcerned he would be should such an event come to pass.

"Not me, Frenchman," boasted Christopher. "I'm not going after the fleet. I'll leave that to the fellows who left earlier. You and I both know that there's always a couple of Spanish stragglers. They'll be scared out there all alone and want to catch up to their fleet as quickly as possible. To do that, they'll have to go the shortest way — through the narrows. And that's where I'll wait for them. I'll just lie there and pick off the stragglers one by one."

Katherine had to admire the man's brain. He appeared to be the only captain who had worked out a strategy. The others had just madly dashed off as soon as they heard the news of the Spanish fleet.

"Are you not afraid of Spanish retribution?" asked Katherine, remembering how Spain had until recently owned most of northern Italy.

"Spain is three thousand miles away and she's rich and lazy. And vulnerable. And an enemy of England. Why, it's patriotic to rob her!"

"I had not heard that Spain was at war with England now," replied Katherine, trying to catch Tom's eyes to see his reaction to this justification.

It was Christopher who answered. "Spain's at war with the whole world in the Caribbean. She's too greedy. She wants all the gold in the New World. Well, the English, French and Dutch want a piece of it, too. And so do I." Nodding toward the silent Tom, he added, "And so do we all."

He caught Katherine's eyes. "There's enough to go around. Even for you, ex-priest. That's why we've come looking for you. To offer you a great opportunity. Think of it. You spend a few weeks at sea and you'll be rich for the rest of your life!"

Katherine looked at him firmly and steadily. "I had been rich before. Before I met you. You stole from me once. Why would I believe you would not steal from me again? I would be a fool to trust you, Captain. And I am not a fool. I want no part of your venture. And no part of you or your thugs."

Christopher showed no reaction to the insult. Matter of fact, he seemed to enjoy it. "But I still have a fancy for music with my meals. And I've already packed the lute aboard. *And your little friend.*"

"What?" Katherine sat up in her chair, alarmed.

"It's true," confirmed Tom, speaking for the first time. "Matto's aboard the *Taingire*."

"And requesting your company," added Christopher, still smiling.

From the look in his eyes she knew he spoke the truth. Matto was aboard the *Taingire*. Through sheer perversity Christopher had figured out a way to get to her. Abduct Matto. If she didn't do as he wished, who knew what hideous things he might do to the man who had saved her life so many times. Once again, he had trapped her. True, she could refuse to go along with him. She had a choice this time. But if she chose not to help Matto, how could she live with herself?

She couldn't.

"All right," she conceded, "I'll go. I'll go with you and play for you and sew for you and man the wheel for you and sing you to sleep each night, if that's where your pleasure lies. But I'll not help you rob or harm any man, and that includes any Spaniards. Though God knows I have no great love of the Spanish throne myself."

"But if you won't share the risk, you won't share the reward," Tom explained to her. He, too, had fallen victim of the gold madness.

"Ah, no, Tom, let him have his way," said Christopher. "One less share means more for you and me. And we've enough fighting men signed on. Maybe, I think, too many."

When Katherine climbed aboard the *Taingire* in late afternoon she saw why Christopher might have reason to worry. She recognized a few familiar faces, among them Bucko and Le Grand, but all looked meaner and more insolent than she remembered. They had regained their health, but apparently lost their ill-gotten wealth in New Providence. Now they had nothing to lose but their lives. That's what made them so dangerous in a fight.

Looking around Katherine wondered if there were any aboard who shared her thoughts. *Will I ever see this island again? Or any island? Or will my dead eyes see only the inside of a canvas shroud as my body is dumped over the side to feed the fishes?*

Nudging her way carefully through the swarms of men milling about the deck, Katherine heard murmurs against Christopher for starting on a Friday.

"Bad luck to start a voyage on a Friday," she heard one brute say.

"Better we wait till Sunday," agreed another.

"But he wants to sail now and he's the captain," responded a third.

"Well, we'll soon see about that," replied the first.

At the sound of the capstan turning, hoisting the anchor, they shut up and Katherine hurried away, seeking Matto. He wasn't on the deck, so they must have sequestered him belowdecks.

Katherine climbed down and immediately stumbled. She could see nothing at first. Her eyes had to adjust from the sea, sky and sun brightness of the deck to the almost total lack of natural light belowdecks.

Once she could see well enough to explore she started down the corridors. And eventually she found Matto. Not tied up and trapped as she had expected. But standing in the storeroom, counting provisions. Katherine looked at him in amazement. He did not look kidnapped, nor abused, only irritated as he marked sums.

"Matto!"

He turned to her with a small cry of surprise and horror. "What are you doing here?"

"I was told you asked for me!" Katherine didn't understand what was going on. "What are you doing? What's going on?"

"No, no, no!" Matto looked truly anguished and frantic. "I told you to remain on the island. You're supposed to remain on the island. I left you a note under the rock by your mat. Did you not see it?"

"I haven't been back to the tent. Christopher brought me directly here from the town." Katherine tried to understand what she was hearing and seeing. "You mean you're here of your own free will?"

"Yes, of course, how else would I be here? As cook, I will receive a half share of all prizes."

Katherine stood in the passageway, dumbfounded, and stared at Matto while it slowly dawned on her what had happened. Christopher had tricked her. Again.

"You've got to get off, Mistress!" said Matto with what sounded more like anger than concern in his voice. "They're sailing with the tide."

Katherine didn't have to be told twice. Up the narrow stairs she went, two at a time, pushing past the knots of men which hampered her at every turn. She broke through into the open air just as the wind caught the newly unfurled sails and the *Taingire* slid through the harbor mouth.

Too late!

Leaning over the rail, looking back at New Providence, she could have cried in frustration. But she checked herself when she became aware of Christopher watching her from the quarterdeck, a large grin on his face. Locking her eyes to his, she vowed that never again, never again would he trick her. Never again would she be on the receiving end of that devilish smile.

She would have her revenge.

Even if it took her the rest of her life.

XVII
PERILS

Christopher dropped anchor off a small island in the Straits of Florida near the Biminis and waited.

For the first week the waiting was not so bad. There was plenty of rum and plenty of food and plenty of high hopes. But after a fortnight had passed without falling in with a vessel of any sort. food started running low. Matto warned Christopher that, because of the great number of mouths to be fed, provisions would not last more than one more week. Christopher immediately dispatched some men in the long-boat to the island but all they could find were a few turtles and birds' eggs.

As the hot summer sun beat mercilessly down, the men started their typical grousing. And what they groused about most was Christopher. The idle malcontents blamed their lack of success on his command. He had sailed too late. He had sailed too early. He had picked the wrong place. He had picked the wrong straits. He had picked the wrong lieutenants.

The tension aboard ship became palpable. When Christopher walked by, whole groups would fall silent before him.

Something had to happen.

Something eventually did.

An accident.

One of the men, a bit dizzy from drinking on an empty stomach in the mid-day heat, fell overboard. His efforts to reclimb aboard gave all on deck a great laugh as they, half-seas over themselves, watched the splashing, sputtering misfortunate. But the hooting and snickering stopped abruptly when a long grey shape suddenly appeared at the man's side.

"Shark!" The cry rang out.

"Quick, a rope!"

"Throw him a rope!"

"Pull him up!"

"Faster!"

But the rope was not fast enough. All that remained at the spot where a man had been flapping about in the light blue sea was a dark red blotch.

In a dead silence the men stood numb at the rail as the blood of their shipmate washed up against the side of the *Taingire*.

Then one finally spoke.

" 'Tis an omen."

"Aye," said another, "an evil omen."

Others also muttered, softly at first, then more loudly as their conviction and tempers intensified. Their voices carried across the deck.

"I knew we should have never sailed on a Friday."

"This is a doomed voyage."

Suddenly a voice shouted down from the helm, louder than any of theirs. "A doomed voyage, is that what I hear you saying?" All eyes turned to the flushed and jubilant Christopher who stood with his legs spread wide on the deck. "Doomed?" he repeated, then pointed to a spot behind the men. "Look there!"

And they did. At once an exultant cry arose from a hundred throats. Gone was their discontent, gone the memory of the shark attack on their fellow man.

A sail had appeared on the Straits! And not a Royal Navy

sail either or that of a small coaster, but the sail of a great Spanish merchantman.

The boatswain whistled and men sprang to action, fairly flying around the capstan to weigh the anchor. Sails unfurled in record time and snapped as they caught the wind.

But the Spaniard had also seen them and tacked under full sail away to the north. Christopher spun the wheel to follow her.

The chase was on! The Spaniard headed for open water. The *Taingire* followed in her wake.

For the rest of that day and all through the moonlit night, the *Taingire* gave chase. Katherine waited and watched and studied the flushed faces of the men around her. She had once been aboard a vessel pursued by men like these. She knew what must be going through the minds of those aboard the Spanish ship. She said a silent prayer for them.

At dawn the Spaniard's luck ran out when the wind shifted and slowly died. Christopher immediately set the *Taingire* on a collision course with his prey while his men primed their courage with bottles of rum and strapped on their muskets, cutlasses, knives and pistols.

When the *Taingire* drifted close enough, Christopher ordered a shot to be fired across the Spaniard's bow. This was the common nautical signal for a ship to strike her colors. Usually the single warning shot sufficed, for the pirates' reputation was so fearsome toward those who resisted them that most ships just submitted in hope of escaping with their lives.

But not this particular Spaniard. She immediately fired back on the *Taingire* with her great 12-pounders.

The fight to the death was on.

Although Katherine carried a knife and pistol herself now, she had no intention of joining in the fight. She retreated belowdecks as the cannons of both ships blasted away at each other with their heaviest guns. *Another nightmare,* thought Katherine, *thanks to Christopher.* She huddled in the hold with Matto as the *Taingire* shuddered and shook. But even the deepest hold was not safe for when the *Taingire* received a broadside, a cloud of oak splinters flew like knives around them. Katherine screamed and cursed Christopher.

As the two ships drifted ever closer together, a volley of small arms fire began to supplement the big guns. When they were at almost point-blank range, the pirates hurled crude grenades onto the deck of the Spaniard. The Spanish soldiers replied with a peppering of iron shot from their swivel guns. And two great shots which blasted open the *Taingire*'s side. Water poured in. The *Taingire* listed and rammed the Spaniard's stern with her bowsprit.

Under heavy fire, the pirates quickly lashed the two impaled ships together. A hundred men scurried up the sides of the Spanish ship like a hundred rabid monkeys. The men knew the *Taingire* was mortally wounded, so they fought with a ferocious desperation, for no Spaniard's weapon could fill their souls with as much terror as the idea of drowning did.

Trumpets and drums, gunpowder smoke, pistol shots, the clashing of cutlasses, Spanish oaths, English oaths, French oaths, all filled the air as the crews slugged it out hand-to-hand. But even over this pandemonium Katherine could make out the groans of the wounded, the pleadings of the maimed, and the screams of those who saw death coming.

The fight raged on for another half hour. In the end, the superior number and fighting skill of the pirates prevailed. When the last cutlass had clanged, when the last pistol had fired, when the last oath had been roared and the last smoke of a musket dissipated, Katherine and Matto cautiously climbed up out of their flooded hideaway to survey the gruesome scene.

What she saw made her sick. The two ships, now wedged together, rocked gently in the soft blue waves. The mainmast of the *Taingire* lay broken in half. The Spaniards' rigging hung loose, cut by a pirate's axe. Shotholes penetrated all wood and sail.

Death and destruction confronted her at each step. Here lay a Spaniard's body, his arm severed from his torso; there lay a pirate's with his face shot off. Those lucky few of the *Taingire* crew who had survived unscathed sat about the deck of their prize in a dazed state of exhaustion, unable to quite believe that it was all over, that they were alive and that they had won.

Katherine saw Tom, his face black with smoke and his hands red with blood, leaning far over the rail. Christopher, blood flowing from a cut over his eye and carrying a bloody knife, roamed the decks, counting the bodies. On the Spaniard's poop deck the Spanish captain stood, motionless, guarded by the pistols of Bucko and the boatswain. A bullet had pierced his ribs but his face registered no emotion.

The only sounds now were the pathetic whimpering of the wounded and the lapping of the waves against the two battered hulls.

Katherine in all her life had never imagined such horror. Hands reached up to try and grab her as she passed by. *"Help me!" "Give me something for the pain!" "God forgive me!"*

As the carpenter who had acted as the *Taingire's* surgeon had been killed, there was no one to tend the wounded but Katherine and Matto and a few fellows who had recovered their wits. They set to work, dressing the wounds of those most likely to survive. The more seriously injured — those with arteries cut or skulls smashed or limbs detached — those were beyond help and were left to die slowly in sticky pools of blood in the mid-day sun.

Katherine reached the far deck by Tom just as Christopher did. She saw the bigger man slap him on the back and turn him around from the railing. "Cheer up, man!" Christopher told Tom. "If you're to be one of us, you'll see many such sights as this. Your first time's always the hardest. You did well, for your first time. You'll make a good fighter, yet."

"No," said Tom hoarsely, shaking his head. "I don't want to be a good fighter. I don't want to fight at all." He seemed about to lose control as he looked around him. "I just killed some of these men. These strangers. With these hands." He looked down at his bloodied and now trembling hands.

"You killed men because if you hadn't, they would have killed you," replied Christopher bluntly. "That's the only thing to remember. A man's got to defend himself, after all."

Then Christopher turned his attention to the matter of the Spanish captain. "Well, captain," he asked, "what think you now of your decision not to strike your colors?"

The Spanish captain, although apparently understanding Christopher's words, chose to spit out his answer in Spanish. Christopher looked around for a translator and spotted Katherine.

"Do you know what he says?" he asked her.

"He says he would rather die than surrender his honor," Katherine answered. She did not translate what the Spaniard had called Christopher.

"Then he shall have his wish," announced Christopher coldly. As he pronounced his sentence, Christopher raised his pistol and shot the captain in the side of the head.

The captain's lifeless body fell.

"As they would have given us no quarter, neither shall we give them quarter!" announced Christopher to his remaining crew.

And thus began the wholesale massacre of the surviving Spanish soldiers.

XVIII
RINGS AND THINGS AND FINE ARRAY

It took several hours to strip all the corpses of their pistols, swords, gold buttons, medals, boots and jewelry. On those hands so bloated in death that the rings could not be easily slipped off, the pirates just hacked off the fingers. The smell of decayed flesh and gangrene hung in the still air. Gulls shrieked and circled in the air above while sharks circled in the sea below. All awaited the carrion feast.

After the men had recovered their wits and stomachs sufficiently, the search of the rest of the *Doña Maria de Toledo* began. While she was not "the Prize" of their dreams — no ship could ever equal their dreams — she still had plenty enough in her to make each man who had survived the battle rich as a colonial governor.

Gold swords, gold doubloons, gold ingots, gold snuff boxes, gold chalices, gold jewelry, all lay below in her hold beside a general cargo of cocoa, tanned hides, tortoise shell, mahogany, and indigo and cochineal dyes.

But the pirates found more than mere cargo belowdecks. The *Doña Maria de Toledo* also carried a full load of passengers bound back to their homes in Spain, petty officials who had amassed enough wealth in the New World to assure their rise in the royal Spanish court.

They were found huddled together in the first mate's cabin like cornered rabbits when the pirate crew kicked the door open. Quickly and brutally the crew herded their find onto the upper deck.

But the greatest surprise awaited the crew in the captain's cabin. There they found a maiden, barely sixteen, with a priest and two serving women. They were all on their knees with their eyes closed, praying madly for a miracle. Or maybe for a quick death.

With a great cry they, too, were prodded and herded up the stairs.

When their eyes adjusted enough to the glare of the sun to make out the slaughter around them, the three women hugged each other and turned their faces. The priest immediately began a Latin incantation.

The appearance of the young lady affected every man on deck. All stopped their plundering and palavering and just stared, open mouthed. Katherine stared too, a feeling of uneasiness rising in her stomach. The girl, a dainty and slender beauty with eyes like black opals, reminded Katherine of Emogena. But the look of terror on the girl's face also reminded Katherine of how she herself must have looked a mere six months before when she was in a similar position.

No one moved. All eyes were riveted on the innocent beauty in the silk mantilla. Then Bucko broke the silence. He gave a whoop and circled her, singing:

I fired me bow-chaser, the signal she knew,
She backed her main tops'l an' for me hove to;
I lowered down me jollyboat an' rowed alongside
An' I found madam's gangway wuz open an' wide.

Then he laughed lewdly and pinched her cheek. She, in turn, did the only thing a well-protected and well-brought-up young lady in her position could do.

She fainted.

What followed happened so fast that later, Katherine

found it hard to remember the precise details although all aboard witnessed it.

As the swooning girl fell, her women ran to attend her.

Bucko knocked the women aside and bent over the small inert body.

The Spanish priest ran up to protest and protect the girl.

Bucko unsheathed his bone-handled steel knife and stabbed the priest in the stomach.

The priest fell, his hands clutching the knife handle sticking out from his stomach.

The maiden groaned, coming to consciousness just in time to see Bucko looming over her, eyes mad with lust.

With one large, filthy, blood-stained hand, Bucko reached out to caress the maiden's throat. With the other hand he reached down to loosen his breeches.

And then Katherine simply walked up behind him, raised her pistol, shot Bucko in the back of the head, and watched as his body fell over the girl's.

At that moment Katherine could not say why she did it, except that, perhaps, it once could have been her lying there. It seemed a dream. She could not believe she could do such a thing. Apparently no one else aboard could believe it either for no one said a word. Tom came up to her and took the smoking pistol from her hand, then placed his arm on hers as if to restrain — or protect — her. But Katherine didn't feel his grip, all she felt was her heart beating.

Then the girl started screaming again, unable to free herself from the weight of the lifeless body of the foul stranger atop her. Christopher gestured for some men to pull Bucko's body off the girl. As son as they did, her women cradled her and tried to hide her face in their ample breasts. But still the girl screamed and moaned and cried.

And the men — particularly Bucko's mates — began to

mutter and slowly move as a group toward Katherine and Tom and the weeping women. Christopher acted quickly to maintain order. He, with studied casualness, strolled between the two groups and turned to face Katherine.

"Well, padre," he declared in a voice that belied the seriousness of what she had done, "I know Bucko here killed a priest which must have upset you some. I'm not one for killing priests myself. I prefer having a little fun with them, taking the wind out of their pompous sails, you know. So I see where you might have a grievance against Bucko. But you signed the *Articles*. And the *Articles* say that all quarrels between men are to be ended on shore."

Katherine, still in a fog, stood mute. It was Tom who spoke in her defense. "Don't the *Articles* also say that if any time a man meets with a virtuous woman and tries to meddle with her without her consent, that man shall suffer present death?"

"Aye, that's true," said Christopher with a nod. A few of the others nodded too. They all knew the rules. "But next time, padre, let's at least vote on it before we kill one of our own. Agreed?"

Katherine nodded.

And so the matter was settled with one last comment from Christopher.

"That's why I've always said, 'No women aboard!' They're trouble-makers all."

Now all attention turned to the captive passengers lined up by the starboard rail. Christopher started pacing up and down in front of them, stopping and starting and making the panic-stricken among them more and more edgy.

Finally one found his tongue when Christopher stopped in front of him to finger the gold chain of office around his neck. "It was good the lady came to no harm," he said in English to Christopher. "She is the only daughter of the governor of

Cartagena. All the Spaniards of Columbia would seek revenge were she defiled."

"Oh, so she's a rich man's daughter, is she?" His interest piqued, Christopher turned for a second look at the wailing girl wedged between the two women in black.

"The only child of the richest man in Columbia. He is sure to pay you well, captain, for her safe return. And for ours, too, of course," the man hastily added. "If you release us all, unharmed, unmolested, I am sure a suitable ransom would be paid."

"Well, now," said Christopher, pondering the information the man had divulged, "there's no doubt in my mind that the richest man in Columbia will pay handsomely for the return of his only daughter. An only daughter cannot be replaced. But," added Christopher, after pausing for effect, "government officials . . . ? Surely government officials are as plentiful as mangoes and papayas in the Cartagena market. I doubt the richest man in Columbia will pay for *your* safe return."

The man blanched at the implication. Christopher just grinned and yanked off his gold chain and threw it on the mound of glittering booty amassing in the center of the deck.

Soon all seven men were stripped down to their shirts and pants. Then Christopher called for what remained of his crew to gather around him. Each man was allowed one vote on what to do with the prisoners. Christopher kept the tally. When each man had had his say, Christopher called over Katherine to translate the verdict.

"My men have decided to show mercy," she translated into Spanish. The Spaniards' faces brightened somewhat. A few even crossed themselves and gave thanks to the heavens. Katherine continued translating Christopher's words. "We will give you your lives and a boat." The Spaniards' faces clouded over again. "If you make it to shore, you can give thanks to Brian Christopher and God. Which, at sea, means the same thing."

The Spaniards exchanged puzzled glances. It seemed their lives would be spared. But why then were the pirates chuckling so?

Katherine found out when the *Taingire*'s long boat was lowered into the water and brought alongside the *Doña Maria de Toledo*. The long boat was riddled with shot holes from the fierce battle. Already two inches of water sat in her bottom. The Spaniards looked at each other in yet more disbelief and despair. "Of course," one of the pirates shouted to them, "you can always swim if you prefer!"

Then, with great guffaws and hoots, the crew proceeded to toss the seven men over the side. They watched gleefully as the Spaniards mauled each other in their efforts to climb inside the leaky vessel and stuff the holes with their shirts. Two grabbed the oars and used them to push the long boat away from the side of the *Doña Maria de Toledo*. All were frantic to get out of firing range as quickly as possible.

"Wait!" cried Christopher to them. "You forgot something!"

Katherine watched as the two screaming attendants were wrenched from the Spanish girl's side. With one man gripping the arms and one the feet, each woman was swung in a wide arc into the sea by the long boat. The Spaniards aboard the boat grabbed hold of the drowning, sputtering women and hauled them aboard.

And the small group rowed into the sunset, a hundred miles from any land, without provisions, without water, without possessions, and without sail.

Katherine did not think they could make it.

The pirates were certain of it.

XIX

TO WATCH THE NIGHT
IN STORMS

After the last body had been stripped and dumped over the side to feed the sharks, after the last of the mortally wounded had given up the ghost, after the last of the coin and curios had been counted and divided, there remained the problem of the two ships.

The *Taingire's* mainmast was broken and her side was ripped with two great holes. The *Doña Maria's* rigging was cut and her topgallants shredded. Plus she had a hole in her gilded stern from where the *Taingire's* bowsprit had rammed her. But that hole, unlike those in the *Taingire*, was far above the waterline.

The pirates had no choice but to abandon the *Taingire* and sail the *Doña Maria*.

So all able-bodied men — and Katherine — set to work transferring sail, rigging, and rope and everything else salvageable from the *Taingire*. When she had at last yielded up everything of value the men disentangled the grappling hooks, hacked her jib off, and set her free. She immediately listed to port — a broken, deserted hulk.

But she didn't sink.

She just lay there, twenty feet away, in the smooth sea. Every now and then one of her old crew would glance at her as he went about his business repairing and restoring the *Doña Maria*. Bets were made on when she would sink.

But with each new dawn, there she was.

After a few days the sight of her seemed to almost irritate

the crew, as if she were rebuking them for abandoning her. So a meeting was called and a vote taken to use her for target practice.

It took ten full rounds of the Spaniards' big 12-pounders to break the obstinate *Taingire*. When the great guns ceased firing, she at last slid quietly under the water. Nothing remained on the spot but a few splintered boards to mark her watery grave.

"Well," some breathed with relief, "now that that is over, we can get on our way."

But most were unaware of one thing, one very important thing. In the week since the battle, a week in which the men feasted, drank, divided their booty, repaired the *Doña Maria* and sank the *Taingire*, in that whole week not one breeze had stirred.

The sea was as smooth as if oil had been poured on it, a fact noticed only by Christopher, Tom, and a few astute older seafarers. While most of the men celebrated and labored oblivious to the weather, these few men would often pause in their labors and examine the sky with concern. Katherine heard an old Scot tell Matto, "When the sea's quiet as a lamb, she's getting ready to roar like a lion."

The rest of the crew only became aware of the weather when the *Doña Maria* had been made as shipshape as it could possibly get at sea. When the *Doña Maria* was ready, the men were ready. But the sails that had just been patched hung loose from the yards like great white dead things. The men cursed as the *Doña Maria* drifted north with the great Gulf Stream. They didn't want to go north, they wanted to go south, back to New Providence to spend their ill-gotten gains.

There was nothing to be done, although almost everyone had a suggestion. A Basque said drowning a cat was the surest way of raising a favorable wind. A Swede claimed a Lapp sorcerer could raise the wind. A Scot claimed that a witch could sell a favorable wind. A Portuguese said that by invoking St. Anthony the wind could be raised.

Christopher scoffed at all their superstitions. He preferred his own. "As we have neither Lapp sorcerers nor witches nor St. Anthony nor cats aboard," he said, "we'll just have to whistle for the wind."

Usually no one was allowed to whistle on board ship for fear of raising a gale. Everyone knew that whistling in a strong breeze might summon up a storm. But they were in such a dreadful humid calm, burning under the hazy sun, that softly, slowly Christopher took the risk and whistled.

Later in the day, when still nothing had stirred, others took to whistling, too. An old salt from Brittany became afraid. He frantically stroked the ivory image of St. Anthony that he wore around his neck and urged the men to stop. "Whistling's a mighty powerful device. It must never be overdone for one can never tell the force of the new wind!"

But the pirates were impatient and ignored his warning. With gold burning holes in their pockets, they whistled and sang and drank and sweated and cursed the dead air and St. Anthony long into the night. "Instead of a cat, let's throw over a dwarf," one joked. And a couple grabbed Matto and lifted him up as if to really do it. It took Christopher, Tom, and a few of the more sober fellows to save Matto. After that close call, Matto quickly scurried below to the comparative safety of the storeroom.

Katherine, too, frequently retired to belowdecks now that she had some privacy there. Since the shooting of Bucko, Katherine had been forced into the role of the young Spanish girl's protector. It was a role she would have never chosen for herself for she found the girl silly, timid, and slow-witted. But the girl had a cabin to herself which she would only open to Katherine.

Katherine had tried to leave the girl under the protection of Tom or Matto. Tom, in particular, was quite taken by the little dark-haired beauty. He would have devoted all his time toward guarding her virtue. But the girl, Francisca de Ayeta, to Katherine's detached amusement, seemed more smitten with Katherine than Tom and clung to her side whenever she was near.

Katherine assured Tom that the girl meant nothing to her, that Francisca only preferred Katherine to him because Katherine could speak with her in her own language. But Tom had observed the girl's eyes light up in Katherine's presence. Such obvious favoritism made Tom peevish. Katherine could only conclude that Tom, a married man turned criminal, was jealous of Katherine, an unmarried woman disguised as a man, because of a witless young girl in whom Katherine had absolutely no interest.

It was all too absurd, thought Katherine as she bolted the door of Francisca's cabin from within as she did every night at the girl's insistence. The only thing more absurd, thought Katherine, was believing that whistling could raise the wind.

Katherine laid down on her narrow pallet and listened to Francisca's steady breathing from across the room. She closed her eyes and tried to block out the oppressive heat, the stale air, the prickly sweat that poured off her body. She tried to sleep. She tried not to hope.

The whistling worked.
During the night the wind did come up.
And up.
And up.

And with the wind came the rain. By noon of the following day the seas had swelled high enough to sweep across the upper decks. At first Christopher tried to outrun the gale. He ordered full sail, and the little *Doña Maria* leapt across the heaving seas.

By late afternoon Christopher realized flight was futile. They would just have to ride out the storm. He ordered the sails to be taken in before they split. Midst the shrieking wind, the hammering rain, the black sky and the surging sea, twelve men struggled to climb aloft and man each yard.

The boatswain, who was responsible for all sails and rigging, tried to shout orders to the struggling men. But his words were swallowed in the wind. Still he tried, holding fast to the rail on the rolling, pitching deck. "Haul away now!" he shouted. Then, seeing the men could still not hear him, he released the rail and, taking a wide stance on the deck for balance, he cupped both hands around his mouth to project his voice. "Up now!" he yelled.

Just then the *Doña Maria* pitched to port, knocking him off his feet and sweeping him through the open rail. Desperate, he grabbed the edge to try and pull himself back aboard. And he might have succeeded, but for the fact that he wore his share of the treasure, a long and heavy gold chain, around his neck. He was a strong man, but his strength was not sufficient to pull both his own weight and the weight of his gold to the relative safety of the deck. He could have cast off his gold chain and maybe saved his life. But he didn't. And so the sea won and carried him off to her.

When Katherine heard the report from one of the eyewitnesses on the yard she wondered why the boatswain did not cast off the gold. She knew he was not a foolish man. Did he not think his life was worth more than a few pounds of gold? Or did he not save himself because he knew he was already doomed by the storm and the sea? Along with the rest of them?

With the sails furled and the yards secured, there was nothing to do for most of the crew now but wait below decks and take their turns at the wheel. Two fellows had to man the helm at all times to prevent the wheel from spinning wildly. One was always either Tom or Christopher, the other any able-bodied man.

By the second day of the storm, four feet of water sloshed in the hold. All hands were called to the pumps, including Katherine and Matto. Crates and kegs and cargo floated across the lower decks. Equipment, provisions, wet powder kegs rattled about in every direction. Rest was impossible. Walking a straight line was impossible. Merely standing in one place was impossible.

Men pumped and prayed and made promises to God.

Around midnight it was Katherine's turn to help man the helm for an hour. Everyone else aboard but Matto and Francisca had already braved the open deck. Katherine, given the choice, figured she would rather die on the open deck than belowdecks, so she did not balk at the duty. And when she climbed the ladder and raised the hatch cover to go on deck, the sight that greeted her indeed convinced her she would die that night.

No one could survive such sea and wind. Waves large as mountains surrounded them. The *Doña Maria* leapt them like a horse gone mad. Katherine was soaked through in seconds. She pulled herself along the rail and bulwarks hand over hand to reach the wheel. Then the sailor she had relieved crawled back the same way she had come. Thus she joined Christopher in his struggle. They stood together, wind roaring in their ears, rain raking their faces, fingers welded to the wooden wheel, along with the gale, the sea, and the pitch-black sky.

As she followed his direction she could occasionally make out his face in the flashes of lightning. He did not look sick with fear as did almost everyone else aboard. He looked almost as if he were enjoying the storm and all its challenges and dangers. She found this attitude almost comforting.

"Have you any hope?" she cried to him over the shrieking wind after one massive wave broke over them.

"I've escaped a thousand storms," he shouted back into her ear. "I was not born to be drowned!"

His supreme confidence in his survival raised her hopes, too, so she tried to match his bravado and answered, "Nay, you were born to be hanged!"

They returned to the battle. Katherine clung to the helm and watched the great walls of water approaching, each of which could be the *Doña Maria*'s last. But the little ship climbed the crest of each one, plummeted into the trough, and climbed again.

Up and down. Up and down.

"The seventh wave's the worst one," Christopher shouted to her.

Katherine couldn't distinguish the first from the seventh in a series. They all looked equally horrible and terrible as they thundered toward her. Each looked fully capable of smashing the *Doña Maria* to bits. Or of capsizing her.

Then the mainyard bent under the force of the wind and broke with a tremendous crash.

"Can we make a safe harbor!?"

"There's no safe harbor in a gale!" he shouted an inch away from her ear as they strained to control the rudder. "Ships sink in harbors, too! We're safer in the open sea! No rocks or reefs to smash open our hull! So we've got to keep her from being pushed west!"

Then came three monstrous waves in succession. On the

third, the tiller snapped and the wheel at which they had been supporting themselves, at which they had been pushing with all their combined strength, gave way.

Immediately both Christopher and Katherine were thrown off balance. They fell to the wet raked deck, Katherine first, Christopher following. Across the pitching wood Katherine slid, unable to grab anything to save her. She saw the edge of the deck come toward her. And she couldn't stop it from coming.

God! she thought, *I am going to die!*

But suddenly, something caught on her vest from behind, stopping her slide. Inch by inch she felt herself being pulled back until she was close enough to Christopher for him to let go of the cloth and clamp his left arm across her breasts and under her armpit. With his right arm he clung to the swinging, torn rigging. They lay together on the rolling deck while the waves pounded their bodies. If his grip weakened or the rope snapped, both would be washed overboard.

Choking from the water she had swallowed, Katherine tried to raise herself up to grab hold of the rigging herself and give Christopher some relief. Finally, largely thanks to Christopher, she reached the line and clung to it though it cut her hands. Then, with Christopher pushing her from behind, she hauled herself along the deck hand over hand to the hatch-cover. There was no sense staying above decks now. No man could help the *Doña Maria*. With no means to steer her, she was totally at the mercy of the gale. She'd go where the wind and waves pushed her.

And it looked as if they might push her straight to the bottom.

XX

WOOING DANCE

For two more storm-wild nights and days the *Doña Maria de Toledo* rolled and quivered and reeled. Her timbers creaked, her masts and yards splintered and crashed, and her hold steadily filled with water despite continual pumping.

But somehow she stayed afloat.

On the morning of the third day a shaft of sunlight broke through the clouds. Ever so gradually the wind and waves waned. The men exchanged glances in the dark, dank hold, afraid to speak their thoughts aloud. Was it their imaginations, or was the wind truly subsiding? Were they at last safe from the storm?

They were. One by one the battered and exhausted men climbed through the hatchcover and into the blessed open air. And face to face with yet another peril.

Land.

Land to the west of them. Land that the *Doña Maria* was heading to straight on. Due to the loss of the tiller, the men could only watch helplessly as the tail end of the gale drove the ship closer and closer to the shore and potential disaster. If there were any shoals, reefs, or rocks off the coast and the waves swept the *Doña Maria* onto them, she would shatter and burst. Her wood had withstood a gale, but it could not withstand the fangs of unyielding stone.

Not a man spoke as they slowly drifted toward the shore. As they edged closer they could see no rocks, but shoals and coral reefs were still a possibility. They looked to Christopher and Tom for guidance. Finally Christopher determined the water was shallow enough and ordered the anchor dropped.

If the line held, they were safe; if the line parted, they were helpless.

The line held.

A cheer went up from the weary crew. Even Katherine felt like crying with relief. She had escaped death once again, she was alive, the gale was over, the sun was shining, and sweet safe land beckoned.

But where were they? she wondered. The stars had not been visible for four nights. Tom reasoned that since the current ran north and the gale blew in from the east, they must be somewhere off the coast of the American colonies, off Florida or Georgia or the Carolinas. He would not be able to tell for sure until the night.

Christopher ordered the longboat dropped and handed the command of the *Doña Maria* over to Tom. He and a group of his best fighting men would row along the coast and explore. As they would need several days, maybe several weeks even, to repair the *Doña Maria*'s tiller and masts, he'd have to find an inlet where she could be towed and turned on her side away from the sight of any passing coastal schooner. He would also check out the inhabitants, for respectable colonial residents might possibly have some objection to the presence of pirates on their land.

By mid-afternoon, the search party had returned and reported. They were not on the shores of America — they were on an island, an island with no sign of recent habitation.

Christopher gave the all-clear signal to disembark. In parties of twelve they rowed to shore. Katherine, Matto, Francisca and Tom were in the last boatload.

As they neared the shore Katherine could see the wrack and ruin caused by the gale. Trees lay on their sides, uprooted. Those that still stood had been stripped bare of foliage. Dead birds and fish and the mashed pulp of rotting fruit lay along the shoreline, stinking in the setting sun.

But despite the devastation before them, not one of the men under Christopher, once on shore, seemed eager to return to the *Doña Maria*. For the first time in almost a month they had solid ground under their feet. The island, they reasoned, might be desolate, but it was in no danger of sinking or cracking up as was the *Doña Maria*.

Once on shore Francisca refused to leave Katherine's side although it had been Tom who had carried the girl through the surf to the dry sand so she would not get her feet wet. But the girl had no reason to fear for her virtue that night, for everyone was so exhausted from their four sleepless days and nights of terror that as soon as the cutthroats' feet touched sand, most just fell over and slept where they fell.

However, the next day was a different story. Awakening to a clear blue sky after a good night's sleep, the men quickly reverted to their original natures and promptly forgot all the sins that they had repented and all the righteous vows they had sworn in the storm. After all, the danger was past, they had no need of God now.

As Matto said, "Vuti di marinaru duranu quantu la tempesta." *A sailor's promises last as long as the storm.*

The next few days were busy ones. Men ferried provisions and powder to shore to dry in the sun, then towed the *Doña Maria* to a lagoon on the north side of the island and beached her. One group took their axes and stripped the branches off the straight trunks of fallen trees to replace the broken masts and yards. Another group patched and tarred the split seams in the *Doña Maria*'s hull. Another group, for which Katherine volunteered in order to get away from the clinging Francisca, reconnoitered the island, seeking fresh water and any edibles which might have escaped the storm's path.

And always a lookout was placed at the bend, for Christopher and Tom had determined from the stars that they were just off the coast of Georgia near a well-travelled shipping lane. If they were discovered by the British Navy or the American militia or even a merchantman cruising offshore, there would be no way to fight or flee with the *Doña Maria* lying helpless on her side.

So, while the sun shone, they worked like the devils most of them were. But when the sun set, their old carefree habits returned. After all, they had much to celebrate, for they had survived so much. Of the approximately 150 men who had left New Providence on the *Taingire*, one had been eaten by sharks, 32 had been killed outright by the Spaniards, 19 had later succumbed to their battle wounds, one had been killed by Katherine, three had been swept overboard during the gale, and one had died of a head wound when he had lost his balance below decks and had slammed against the mizzenmast.

No one mourned these lost companions. For the less the total number, the bigger the individual share.

Katherine, as usual, tried to hold herself aloof from the rest. She set up her makeshift bed at some distance down the beach. And where she went, Francisca followed. And where Francisca went, Tom followed. And so these three ate together, slept together, and waited together. In truth it was a good thing that Tom did stay close to Francisca, especially when Katherine showed no interest in her company and wandered off. For when the men had recovered their energy and itchiness they remembered a woman was in their midst. If Tom had not been there to protect her, they surely would have taken advantage of the young girl.

But Tom had earned their respect during the gale with his

bull-dog tenacity. So they steered clear of "his woman." And because that's how the men around them now thought of Francisca, that's how Tom began to think of her, too. Francisca, on her part, seemed willing enough to let Tom love her but she obstinately refused to grant him the slightest favor. With every hour spent by his olive-skinned, black-eyed beauty, he fell more and more in love. But for the girl's obvious favoritism toward Katherine, Tom might have been perfectly contented on the island.

Katherine, in the meantime, had been exploring. And listening. And thinking.

An idea began forming in her head, an idea which might mean deliverance from all her problems. It involved risk, but Katherine had finally learned that little in life didn't involve risk. After all, if she hadn't been willing to take a risk, she would now be Signora Cesaro Benno of Verona.

The risk involved Tom, because her plan depended on him. Matto had told her so long ago never to trust anyone. Did she dare trust Tom?

Katherine weighed her choices. She could choose to trust Tom, he could choose to join in her plan, she would gain all. She could choose to trust him, he could choose to betray her, she would lose all. Or she could choose not to trust him, give up her plan, and she would be no better or worse off than she was now.

She decided to trust him. One step at a time. She'd test him first.

The evening of their fifth day on the island as the three took their meal, Katherine casually asked Tom, "How far do you think we are from the coast of the mainland?"

"About twenty miles," he answered.

"That's not a great distance."

"No, it's not."

"It's actually within rowing distance, isn't it? One could, if one wanted to, actually row it, couldn't one?"

Tom looked at her. "It could be rowed by a man with strong arms and a strong will in a sturdy boat. Why?" he asked, suddenly suspicious.

"Just wondering if you think it could be done." Katherine backed off.

"Certainly it could be done. If we truly are just twenty miles from the coast. But we might be thirty or forty or fifty."

"Then one would need more than one pair of strong arms. Or one would need someone along who knew how to rig a sail. If one were to attempt such a thing."

Katherine could see Tom reflecting while he studied the figure of the girl opposite him. Francisca smiled at them both, not comprehending any of their conversation but liking the attention. Katherine deliberately intruded on his thoughts. "I imagine," she suggested, "that whoever brings the señorita home safely, whoever rescues her, will not only be handsomely rewarded but will surely be pardoned by the Spanish crown for any transgressions he may have committed to effect her rescue."

"What do you mean?"

She now had his full attention. "I mean anyone of us could rescue the girl and expect a proper reward. The girl would certainly speak in his favor."

"Speak in *your* favor you mean."

"No, Tom. I mean speak in *your* favor." It was now or never. She decided to take the risk. She deliberately lowered her voice. "You know what I'm talking about, Tom. Do you want to spend the rest of your life with the likes of them?" Katherine gestured back toward the pirate campsite. "Killing and robbing? And maybe being killed yourself? Or even worse yet, captured? Brought back to England in chains to be tried and found guilty and hung from a gibbet on a bridge for all to see? To swing there in the sun while the gulls pick away your rotting flesh?

"Isn't that how you've told me your English deal with pirates?"

Tom had turned pale at her words.

"Yes," he admitted hoarsely, "that's true. When I was a child, I remember my father pointed out Kidd's body to me. They'd hung him at Tilbury Point so anyone sailing in and out of the Thames could see him. They'd dipped his body in tar and bound it in metal straps and hung it from a chain. I remember it swayed in the breeze.

"I remember it was awful."

He shivered, remembering. "I . . . I couldn't stand that," he said. "I'll die by my own hand first before I'll let them do that to me."

Katherine grabbed hold of his upper arm. "Tom," she said, flushed and stern, "I'm telling you you don't have to die like that! I'm telling you you've got a chance here to get out! *Listen to me.* Tonight, after they all drink themselves into a stupor like they always do, you, me, and the girl can escape in the longboat. With the *Doña Maria* beached, there will be no way for them to catch us. It's a perfect plan. We'll be free of them at last!"

"Free at last," Tom echoed with a spark of life at last in his eyes. But then the spark died and he shook his head. "I've made such a mess of my life, I shall never be free. I can never escape my past."

"I have," said Katherine simply.

And she took a deep breath and told him her story.

XXI

WOMANLY PERSUASION

Shaking his head in amazement at her revelation, Tom uttered the words Katherine had gambled her secret on to hear: "All right, I guess if you could pull that off, you could pull off anything. I'll go with you."

Then, point by point, they fine-tuned their plan. Tonight she, Tom, and Francisca would steal away in the longboat and make for the coast of America.

Katherine considered asking Matto to join them although, after the gale, he had vowed to stay on shore the rest of his life. But many made that vow when the sea was heaving and most had promptly forgotten it when the sea was sparkling and peaceful as it was now.

But Katherine had observed that Matto seemed content in the pirate's company. After all, he had willingly deserted her on New Providence to join the group when they sailed off in their quest for "the Prize." Katherine did not condemn him for the act for, without her wealth, she had little to offer him. The day seemed far off when she could retrieve the ruby necklace from the forest of New Providence. Matto owed her nothing. She owed him nothing. Both were free to act on their own now.

But Katherine had waited too long to act.

By cautiously putting off her approach to Tom, she had ignored his earlier words of advice aboard the *Mag Mell*: "He that will not sail till he have a full fair wind, will lose many a voyage."

For just as she and Tom were agreeing on the final details of the plan, around the bend the pirates were righting the *Doña Maria* to float her out with the evening tide. They had four hours of summer sunlight left, plenty of time to load her up and sail before the tide ebbed.

Katherine, stung to the quick when Matto came to tell them the news, exchanged an agonizing glance with Tom. The four quickly got up and hurried to the lagoon. When they reached the knoll above it, their own eyes confirmed Matto's report. The *Doña Maria* did indeed appear fit enough to sail. Christopher and his men had done a good job of repairing her.

Katherine whispered to Tom. *"You've got to do something!"*

Tom nodded, then climbed atop a rock near the men laboring about the beached *Doña Maria*. "Now wait a minute," he shouted to them. The men, always eager to take a break, stopped what they were doing and turned to him. "Just hold it up now," Tom continued now that he had their attention. "I think we're going about this all too fast. We shouldn't take her out without testing her seaworthiness first! And we certainly shouldn't take her out at night first.

"As the quartermaster, I say we wait till tomorrow. Why, she's not dried out yet. She doesn't look all that fit to me."

A look of concern crossed over the faces of some of the crew — especially those who were more used to fighting than sailing. One contrary fellow decided to challenge Tom. "How would you know how she looks? You've looked at nothing but the lady all week!"

The others around him laughed and nodded their heads in agreement.

Tom flushed and tried to get their attention back. "True, I have not inspected her . . . ."

"You mean the lady?" another voice called out. The men

once again broke into lewd laughter.

Tom ignored him and tried again. "I have not inspected the *Doña Maria* closely but I know that five days ago there were six feet of bilge water in her bottom." Some of the men nodded. "Listen. We've nothing to lose by waiting for morning. We'll take her out and anchor her now. If she's still floating high and dry by morning's light, then we'll be sure of her fitness. Remember, it's a good 500 miles to New Providence and the current's against us. Do you want to risk her sinking under you a hundred or so miles out at sea?"

Katherine could see that most of the men were weighing Tom's words. Her hopes rose. Now if only Tom could get them to vote on a delay . . .

"After all," added Tom, "what matter is twelve more hours? If we wait, we'll not only be assured of her soundness, but we'll get a good night's rest for the voyage home!"

Seduced by the image of sleeping one more night in the soft sand and fragrant air, instead of packed into the hard floor of the fetid hold, most of the men nodded. Tom had convinced them. He smiled at his triumph.

But he had reckoned without Christopher. The dark captain, who had been sitting to the side of the group quietly listening and smoking, now stood up and tapped his pipe against a rock.

"I'll tell you what matter twelve more hours is, Englishman," he shouted over to Tom. "That's twelve more hours for a naval ship to spot us. The gale's long over. The coastal patrol's sure to have started up again. This island's too damn close to civilization and its navies and its laws for me."

Now head nodded in agreement with Christopher's words. The consensus shifted yet again.

"If you can give me a good enough reason for waiting

that's worth risking a British Navy gibbet, I'll wait the extra half day. But it's got to be better than what you've come up with. The *Doña Maria*'s in no danger of sinking. She got us through a gale all right, didn't she?

"I think you're just eager for another tropical night under a full moon with your lady. Why, man, you can have plenty of those on New Providence!" And with a sly smile he added, "Or, if you'd like, we can maroon you two turtle doves here. Then you can bill and coo all you please until you happily die in each other's arms."

Tom blushed under his sunburn as the men hooted and laughed. Insults to himself he could bear. Insults to his chaste lady he could not. Katherine thought he would strike Christopher. So did the men between them who quickly stepped back to clear a path between the two antagonists.

No one spoke. The only sound was that of the waves lapping gently at the edge of the lagoon. The two men faced each other down. The taller, fine-boned, fair-haired Englishman against the shorter, broad-shouldered, dark-haired Irishman. Christopher, with the assurance accrued from a hundred such confrontations, waited for Tom to make the first move. But Tom seemed to be struggling within himself. If he fought Christopher and won, the men would listen to him and delay sailing and he could proceed with his plan of escape. But if he fought Christopher and lost, not only would they all sail at midnight, but his position of authority would be forever undermined.

He glanced at Francisca who, even in her ignorance, sensed something of import was taking place. Katherine knew what he was thinking. If Tom lost a fight with Christopher — and lost his stature with the crew — he could no longer command the right to protect her. She would be at their mercy. And, Tom knew well, they had no mercy.

His first duty must be to her. And if that meant backing down to Christopher and giving up the escape plan, then he'd back down and give it up.

He caught Katherine's eye and shrugged as if apologizing. Then he simply turned his back on Christopher and walked away.

Christopher had won. Again.

"All right, let's get on with it!" Christopher ordered and the men resumed their loading.

Katherine stood immobile. She couldn't stand it, wouldn't stand it. She stared at the swaggering figure of Christopher. This was the man responsible for thwarting her grand scheme. This was the man responsible for her presence on the *Doña Maria*, for her presence on the *Taingire*. This was the man who had robbed her, who had abducted her, who had used her.

As she stared at him, the source of so many of her frustrations, a hard core of rebellion fired her brain. True, she had no position, no money, no jewels, no family, no friends. It seemed as if she possessed nothing of power to bargain with, nothing of sufficient value in his eyes that would induce him to delay the sailing.

Except for one thing.

All her life Katherine had rued being born a woman. All her life she had blamed all her troubles on that one fact. All her life that one fact had thwarted her from getting what she thought she wanted. But now, now what she had considered to be her greatest liability might turn out to be her greatest — not to mention her only — asset. A curse could be, in certain circumstances, a blessing.

It was worth a chance.

And so Katherine took a deep breath and strode up to Christopher. "You asked for a reason to stay on this island another night. Well, I'll give you a good reason, captain." He raised a skeptical eyebrow. She lowered her voice so no one could overhear them. "Come to the center of the island with me tonight and I'll show you something that might interest you."

Katherine boldly looked into Christopher's coldly amused eyes. He did not reply, but he did not turn away. Did he remember the night they were almost swept overboard? The night he wrapped his arm around her body to pull her back from the raging surf? Had he felt the small soft breast through her thin wet shirt and guessed her secret? And if he hadn't, had she just piqued his curiosity enough for him to leave his cronies and follow her into the center of the island?

She waited, refusing to lower her eyes.

Finally he nodded. "All right," he said. "I'll go with you. I'll see if what you have to show is worth missing the tide for and risking my neck."

Katherine breathed a sigh of relief. One hurdle overcome.

Christopher turned to his men and announced, "I'm going off for a wee bit. If I'm not back in a couple hours, do as the Englishman said and see if she floats. If she does, we'll weigh anchor tomorrow noon." Then, turning back to Katherine, he grinned and said, "Lead the way, *padre*."

So he did know, thought Katherine.

She started on ahead, he grabbed a bottle of brandy from the stash on the beach. *That's good,* she thought, *I'm going to need it to get through the next few hours.* It was six o'clock, low tide. The sun would not set nor the moon rise for another three hours. The tide would be at its height around midnight. So she would have to keep him occupied for at least two hours after midnight. Then she and Tom and Francisca could sneak away.

But eight hours was a long time to keep a man's attention.

As her father's shrewish daughter in Padua she had scarcely been able to keep any male guest's attention for eight minutes. Why hadn't she listened more carefully to Signorina Lupe's lessons in the arts of coquetry?

How could she seduce someone when she knew almost nothing about the art of seduction?

XXII

FIRST ENCOUNTER

Katherine kept the pace leisurely as they tramped inland past the dunes with their clams and turtle tracks, past the marshes with their mosquitoes and snakes, and into the forest with its shady cypress and mossy oaks. The island was beginning to recover from the effects of the gale. The hawks and eagles and egrets and herons had returned and sang and screeched in the setting sun. The air was balmy with the scent of flower and fern. To Katherine's relief Christopher did not try to rush her nor did he disturb her thoughts with questions or comments.

Finally, after almost an hour, they stopped by the pool that fed the island's only stream. Katherine had discovered it on one of her exploratory hikes. She knew there was no sense walking further, they would just reach the opposite shore if they kept on. So she simply stopped and turned to Christopher. Awkward and silent, she pointed toward the west where the sun was setting and turning the sky into orange and red and purple.

" 'Tis a beautiful spot," said Christopher.

"Yes," agreed Katherine, uncertain as to how to proceed.

"But 'twas a great long walk to get to it."

Katherine, in her discomfort, could think of no response.

"And I don't think you brought me all this way just to show me the view. After all, you never invited me to see the view from your hill in New Providence."

"No," admitted Katherine. *Fool*, she said to herself, *keep talking! Then you won't have to do anything!* So she tried to act at ease and speak in a normal tone. "No, I have to admit New Providence has a better view from her coral hills than this low-lying island does from here. In fact, New Providence has all the makings of an Eden, don't you think? Plenty of fresh water and food . . ."

"Plenty of hurricanes and gnats," he interrupted as he sat down by the banks of the pool, removed his shoes, and dangled his feet into the water. "I hope now, . . ." he paused and looked up at her. "By the way, just what is your name?"

"Antonio."

"No. I mean your *real* name."

So he knew. He probably always knew.

"Katherine," she answered.

"Katherine," he repeated with satisfaction. "That's a pretty name. I knew a Katherine once in Port Royal. Well now, Katherine, as I was saying, I hope you're not one of those deluded souls who gets hoodwinked by the island life, thinking that because life there looks easy, it must therefore be easy." He padded the moss beside him. "Come on, sit down here beside me so I don't have to keep looking up, and I'll tell you the bloody truth."

She sat, stiffly and warily.

He rested back on his elbows. "You can starve just as easily on a beautiful tropical island as you can on a cold rock in the North Sea. Starving is starving, no matter where you are. There's only one thing that keeps a body from starving. And that's money."

"Do you see money as the answer to all your problems, Captain Christopher?"

"Yes I do," he admitted. "And if you don't, that tells me you're either a fool or you've never had to worry about where your next meal's coming from. I don't think you're a fool, Katherine. Although thinking you can pass yourself off as a man is certainly a fool thing."

"But it's worked," retorted Katherine stubbornly.

"Until now, it's worked," he challenged.

"Until now, it's worked," she conceded.

"Yes. Well, that's the great mystery now, isn't it? If it's worked so bloody well until now, why are you suddenly tossing it over . . . just for me?"

"I thought you always knew," she lied, as simply and innocently as she could.

"I had my suspicions I'll admit. I've learned to suspect all smooth-cheeked lads. You know you aren't the first woman to try and change her sex. I've met a few on other ships. And heard of several more. But you're different from them. They did it to follow their sweethearts or to escape the law or to earn a dishonest living without having to spread their legs.

"But you, you're high-born, aren't you? You play the lute and harpsichord. You know Latin and Greek. You have a dwarf servant. You *had* a dwarf servant, that is. Now all that tells me you must have had a pretty easy life wherever you were. So why would a rich woman give up that easy life, change into a man's clothes, and take off across the great sea? Tell me that."

"I was to be married." Katherine had no reason for hiding that truth. It was curiously pleasant simply to sit there, quietly and at last speaking the truth. Christopher had made no move to harm her, nor spoken any words to hurt her. Yet.

"So you were to be married? What of it? Sounds natural."

"I did not wish to be married."

"Ah," he smiled. "A woman who does not wish to be married. Now that is indeed a remarkable woman! Tell me how you came to develop such an extraordinary perversity."

So she told him her story, stretching out the details until the last rays of the sun had disappeared in the west.

When she had finished, he looked at her with a bemused interest. "Well, that's quite a little adventure you've had. I like a woman who knows her own mind, who's willing to take a chance, who's a little bit dangerous because of it."

Then he took her hand in his and drew it to his lips.

So now it begins, she thought.

"Come to me, Katherine. It's time you became a woman again."

And so she let him pull her down to his side, and let him press his mouth on her mouth, his flesh on her flesh. She could feel her heart pounding. Slowly he unbuttoned both her shirt and breeches and began exploring her body with his hands. Katherine felt fear run like a fever through her blood. But when she finally lay naked on her wilderness bed and felt the full weight of Christopher's body on hers, she also felt a rush of pleasure after the first shock. Christopher's breathing quickened but he did not say anything. Her breathing almost stopped but she couldn't say anything.

Alarmed at her body's reaction, Katherine forced herself to open her eyes and stare up at the palm-fringed indigo sky as the full moon rose and the first stars appeared. She tried to keep her mind clear by counting the stars over and over.

Until it was over.

Already?

Before Katherine knew what was happening Christopher rose up off her, then drew up his breeches and rolled over on his back. With his left arm he pulled her over to him so that her head rested in the crook of his arm.

Was that it? Katherine looked at him. His eyes were closed. She could see his chest rise and fall steadily.

He had fallen asleep.

Katherine was wide awake. And amazed at what she had just experienced. She replayed it in her mind and tried to figure it out as she lay by his side and listened to him breathe. This was not what she had expected. She had expected it to be a terrible thing. That was what her mother and Signorina Lupe had indicated all those years. But Katherine did not find it so terrible. And that, according to what her family and religion had taught her, must mean that she was a terrible person. Only a terrible person would enjoy a terrible thing.

Katherine lay still for a half hour, an hour, two hours, until near midnight when the moon rose high above her. Its brightness silhouetted all about her in a blue light. She could see everything perfectly — the trees, the glade, the pool . . . Christopher's face, Christopher's body, Christopher's knife.

The moonlight glinted off the silver steel of the blade Christopher wore on his right hip. Its sparkle bewitched her, it seemed to be inviting her to touch it.

It was, after all, within reach of her left hand. All she had to do was reach out, ease it from its leather sheath, lift it high, and then plunge it deep into the exposed vitals of the sleeping man by her side. She could then run back down to the beach, rouse Tom and Francisca, and escape. The three would be long gone by the time the fuzzy-brained cutthroats discovered their disappearance and Christopher's body and connected the two.

Yes, she could kill him. Easily. And if she killed him, the man with whom she had done the terrible and wonderful thing, maybe she could redeem herself.

Maybe that was what the glittering knife was telling her.

Just reach for it.

Reach for the silver steel.

An inch at a time she eased her left arm down his chest, pausing frequently to check that his breathing remained regular and deep. She felt sweat break out over her body. Another inch. Was his breathing becoming more shallow? She froze. Then scolded herself, *It's your imagination.*

Another inch, and another.

Finally the tips of her fingers passed from the warm soft flesh of the living man to the cold hard steel of the lethal instrument. She raised her head slightly from his shoulder to see better and slowly, ever so slowly, drew the blade.

When at last she had it free she lifted it over the man who had that night violated her — at her own invitation — and then cradled her. She gripped the knife handle so tightly that she could see the veins of her wrist standing out. Her hand started to tremble under the strain. She licked her dry lips. Here was her golden opportunity, she would probably never get another chance like this one. Why was she hesitating?

Do it! she ordered herself.

XXIII

TWO RAGING FIRES

But she didn't.

And when she didn't, a hand, swift and easy as a cat, flew up and seized her wrist, then turned it so that the sharp blade pointed harmlessly up to the sky.

Taken by surprise, she cried out.

"Now you wouldn't be thinking of using my own knife on me, would you? After we've just had the most pleasant of evenings?"

Christopher flicked Katherine's wrist so hard that her hand opened and the knife fell to the moss. He proceeded to quote the Finistere proverb to her, more with amusement than anger. " 'However treacherous the sea may be, women are even more treacherous.' "

Both sat up. Christopher retrieved the knife, cleaned it on his breeches and casually replaced it in its sheath. Katherine pulled her clothes back on and tried to understand what had just happened. Curiously, for someone who had almost been murdered in cold blood, he neither raged nor retaliated. Curiously, too, Katherine felt no fear of him now. Even though he might kill her now and call it justice. Maybe she had been through too much that night to feel any more. Or maybe, because she'd just held his life in her hand, he no longer seemed so omnipotent, so invincible, so over-whelming. For the first time, she felt his equal. And at peace.

He sensed the change in her. All bullying was gone from his voice and manner. He seemed puzzled by her serenity.

"Well, Katherine? You had your chance, why didn't you take it?"

"I was thinking of it," she admitted. "But I couldn't do it. I'm no murderer."

Christopher leaned back on his elbow and raised one eyebrow. "I seem to recall you murdering old Bucko right easily. And with nary a pang of tender conscience."

"Oh," she replied. She had conveniently forgotten all about that. "That was different. That wasn't deliberate."

"Oh, wasn't it?" he questioned with sarcasm.

"No," she bristled indignantly. "It wasn't. At least, it wasn't like the way you murdered the Spanish captain."

"The Spanish captain asked for no quarter and I gave him none." This time she raised her eyebrow at his explanation. But he seemed to want her to understand, so he continued, "Katherine, he was bound to die. A swift death by my hand or a slow death at the hands of the men. The men like slow deaths, you know. Remember the mate on the *Mag Mell*?"

Katherine remembered and shuddered.

"Now you, Katherine, you thought for a long while whether to plunge that knife into my belly. Didn't your religion tell you that the thought was as bad as the deed? That thinking about killing a man is as bad as killing him? Of course from my point of view, that is to say the point of view of the intended victim, there's a whole world of difference between the two."

He smiled for the first time. "I'm glad you didn't kill me, Katherine. Now maybe we can get some real sleep."

"I thought you were asleep before," she said.

"With you at my side all shaking and quivering like the Jolly Roger in a north wind? I'm not deaf, dumb, and blind, girl. And I'm not stupid. You did not invite me up here because you were crazy with love for me and you just had to satisfy your passion. I always knew you had some scheme. I was just playing along, waiting to see how the cat jumped.

"So what is your scheme, Katherine?"

"I just did not want you to sail tonight."

"I figured out that much. But why not?"

"We're close to the American coast, aren't we?"

"Aye, too close."

"I was going to steal the longboat tonight and row west."

"By yourself!?" He scowled in disbelief. "It's a good twenty, thirty miles across a swift-moving current. With your skinny arms, you couldn't row five miles!"

"You'd be surprised at what I can do when I make up my mind."

"Oh no, I wouldn't." He shook his head. "You're a strong-minded woman, Katherine, and an enterprising one, too. But you'll never convince me that you intended to pull this off by yourself." With his fingertips, he started softly stroking the hairs on her exposed lower arm. But the smile was gone from his eyes and the amusement gone from his voice when he next spoke.

"So who of my crew has turned traitor? Who of my crew was going to steal my longboat and row off with you?"

Katherine didn't know whether her skin prickled because of his touch or because of the sudden ominous tone in his voice. Still, she remained calm as she answered, "I swear to you that this was totally my idea. I conceived it. I planned it. And I intended to do it. No one else is responsible."

"Not even the dwarf?"

"Not even he."

He removed his hand from her arm. "Well, you've got loyalty at least. I'll give you that much."

Using his palms for a pillow, he entwined his fingers, laid back on the moss and studied the stars. She remained a few feet away from him and studied him.

"Truly, Christopher, I mean you no harm anymore."

"Not even for what I did a couple hours ago?"

He stopped looking at the stars and looked directly at her. This time she looked away as she answered with the truth.

"No," she said.

Then she turned back to him. "All I want is to escape this life I'm caught in with you. Remember, I did not freely choose it, as you did. You chose it for me, on the *Mag Mell*, when you abducted me, and then again on New Providence when you tricked me onto the *Taingire*. I want to be free of you, of your men, of everything connected with your way of life. It's no way of life for me."

She paused and waited for him to answer. When he didn't, she decided to ask the most important question of all.

"So will you let me go?"

He remained silent. So she played with the ferns at her feet and waited.

Finally he sat up, cleared his throat and took a deep breath. He was ready to speak his piece.

"Do you think you're the only one who wants out of the life?" he began. "This life you say I chose, that I could argue chose me, may tempt Providence at times, but damn it all, it does stir the blood of a man! And I have always thought the rewards were well worth the risk. But in the past year or two, when the rewards have been so few and the risks so many, I've begun to have my doubts.

"All the great ones of the life — Morgan, Every, Kidd, Bonnet, Tew — where are they now? I'll tell you where they are. Dead, diseased, or swinging from an Admiralty gibbet! I've sailed with a lot of men, Katherine, who wound up with nothing but a rough noose around their necks. And those that escape the noose still have to bear up against ship's fever, starvation, dysentery, scurvy, foul weather, cannon shot, bullets, knives, fists, maggot-infested bread, poisoned fish, and the pox.

"I've had lots of men die in my arms at sea. And I've watched their bodies chucked overboard without so much as a paternoster.

"That's not the way I want to go. I want a few words said when I go. And a few tears shed.

"Picture those men waiting for us back on the beach, Katherine. There's probably not eight of them over thirty years of age. I'm thirty-seven, an old man to them.

"Oh, it's a young man's life all right.

"When I was fourteen, my death meant nothing to me. And when I was nineteen, after five years of the living death of an indentured servant, there were times when I would have welcomed a clean permanent death. From nineteen on, during all those years of privateering and pirating, death was a part of the dues. I just accepted it and didn't really think too much about it. But then again I never figured I'd make it to thirty.

"Well, I made it to thirty. I even made it to thirty-five. And now I'd kind of like to make forty. Fifty even.

"Look at me, I'm starting to take on a paunch! I used to be all muscle and bone! Ah, Katherine, I tell you it's high time for me, too, to get out. And settle down. And maybe even marry some wild and doughty lass who'll give me a good run." He grinned, caught her eye, then deliberately ran his eyes up and down her body. For the first time that night, she blushed.

To ease her discomfort, she spoke. "In New Providence they said that Governor Rogers is offering a king's pardon for all men who forswear piracy."

"I heard that too. But now that I've made enough money, I

don't need a pardon. All I was waiting for was a big enough prize. And now I've got it. The rest of the crew down there, why they'll just drink and gamble and whore until every last doubloon has dribbled through their fingers. In two months they'll wonder where it all went. And they'll have to put out to sea again. And again. Always working for the gold.

"Well, not me. Not any more. I intend to make the gold work for me. Isn't that the way the rich work it? You're a rich man's daughter, you would know."

"I know very little of where my father's money came from," Katherine confessed.

"See there. Only a rich man's daughter could afford to be so ignorant. Now I bet you know better."

"Yes," said Katherine wryly. "Thanks to you I've not only gotten a whole lot smarter, I've gotten a whole lot poorer, too."

He ignored her acerbic accusation. "All I have to do now is arrange my demise. I've got it all figured out. I'll go to London, much as I hate the dark, dirty place, and I'll find some disease-ridden pauper on his last legs. I'll offer to give him a decent burial in exchange for his name. Then Brian Christopher, the notorious pirate, will be dead. All charges against me will be dropped and forgotten. I'll turn myself into an honest Englishman. I'll have a new name and be free to live a new life. I'll be a planter in the New World."

"You, a planter?" Katherine couldn't picture it.

"And why not? I heard once of a planter on Barbados who turned pirate. So can't a pirate just as easily turn planter?

"I've learned of a plantation outside Port Royal on Jamaica that's up for sale. I've even put in an anonymous bid on it. Fine place, rich soil. I'll grow sugar, cacao, indigo, cotton, even my own tobacco for my own pipe. And there's a garden with grapes and oranges and cabbages fresh for my dinner table. No guest of mine will ever go hungry.

"And if I feel like hunting there's game fowl and wild pigs in the woods. And if I feel like fishing there's fresh-water springs aplenty." He smiled and sighed at the vision. "But more than likely I'll just spend my days stretched out in a hammock strung between two palms, fanned by a sea breeze and sipping from a glass of brandy that never runs dry. My only worry will be deciding which silks to wear to dinner."

With his eyes closed, and with a beatific smile on his face, he completed painting the picture of his future. "And I'll die old and drunk in the strong soft arms of my lady-love."

He opened his eyes and caught hers. "Does that appeal to you, Katherine, my lady-love?"

"Does it appeal to me to have an old drunk die in my arms, is that what you're asking?"

"You know what I'm asking."

She avoided answering by asking a question of her own. "Since when am I your lady-love?"

"Since you seduced me and stood up to me and didn't knife me when you had the chance."

"That hardly seems a basis for love."

"It's good enough for me! So here's what you must do. You must wait for me. Now I know you're a high-born expensive lady and I'm . . ."

". . . a son of a bastard's bitch," finished Katherine.

He laughed. "Where did you learn that expression?"

"It's what I heard you called aboard the *Taingire*."

"Well, I suppose it's as good a way as any to describe me. But in six months I'll be a proper gentleman. And I'll need a proper wife.

"Am I moving too fast for you now, Katherine? Then pay attention. I've told lots of girls I'd marry them before I bedded them. You're the first I've asked after. You're no ignorant girl, Katherine, like the Spanish lass, who'd play the fool and sigh and whine for her mother if I laid a hand on her."

Katherine protested, "I did not lie with you tonight for marriage, nor money, nor love."

"But you could love me, if you made up your mind to," he said, both wooing and mocking her. "You must love me, Katherine, for I need a strong mate like you who'll not knife me in the night.

"We're a good match for each other. And you know it. I knew I'd have to meet my match some day, but never in my wildest dreams did I imagine anyone like you."

"So tonight your wildest dream has come true?"

"Has yours?" he asked intensively.

She did not answer. But she was asking herself the same question.

"Well? Do you want me to pay court to you first, is that it? Is that why you're not answering me? All right then, I can do that. I know how to play that game . . .

> "Prithee Chloe, not so fast,
> Let's not run and Wed in haste
> We've a thousand things to do,
> You must flye, and I persue;
> You must frown, and I must sigh;
> I intreat, and you deny.
> Stay — If I am never crost,
> Half the Pleasure will be lost;
> Be, or seem to be severe,
> Give me reason to Despair;
> Fondness will my Wishes cloy,
> Make me careless of the Joy.
> Lovers may of course complain

Of their trouble and their pain;
But if pain and Trouble cease,
Love without it will not please."

Katherine remained silent. This night had been filled with too many surprises for her to express her thoughts clearly. Christopher, in turn, interpreted her silence as reluctance and made one final proposal.

"All right, then. I'll tell you what I'll do to prove to you I mean what I say.

"I'll help you escape tonight."

"What?" she asked in amazement.

"I'll help you escape tonight," he repeated, "if you'll give me your troth. Give me your troth and six months to settle things in England. I'll give you some coins and you can make your way to Port Royal — I've no doubt you can make your way anywhere — and I'll meet you there in six months."

Then he took both her hands in his and pulled her over to him.

"I know what I want, Katherine. I've always known what I wanted. I wanted gold and I found it. I wanted my own land, and I found it. And I wanted a fine woman, and I found you. You belong to me now, Katherine, for I know you now. And I want you. I've never wanted another woman the way I want you.

"Come to me, Kate. Kiss me."

XXIV

LIFE AND LIBERTY

Christopher kept his word.

Just before dawn when the two returned to the inlet, Christopher moved to secure the longboat while she aroused Tom and Francisca. Tom, surprised that the plan was still on, was even more surprised at the spectacle of Christopher's collusion. Wisely, he asked no questions.

They had no time to lose for the moon was low in the west. Dawn would break in less than an hour. Carefully, they edged their way past the sleeping, snoring bodies. The only other sound was that of the breaking surf. When they reached the longboat without rousing anyone, Tom threw in their satchels and gestured for Katherine and Francisca to climb inside. Then the two men pushed it from the strand to the foam to the swelling waves. As soon as the small vessel floated free, Tom scrambled aboard. Christopher, wet to the waist, retreated to the shore to watch.

Tom quickly handed the port oar to Katherine and took the starboard one for himself. Once past the breakers, they began rowing west — away from the rising sun, away from the island and the *Doña Maria*, and away from Christopher. As Katherine had to face backwards to row, every time she raised her eyes she could see the figure of Christopher standing on the beach, watching. Even when the island itself finally began to recede into the rising sun, in her imagination Katherine still saw him standing there, watching.

Lift. Dip. Pull. Recover. Repeat.

Lift. Dip. Pull. Recover. Repeat.

Hour after hour after hour.

Katherine's back began to ache and her palms to blister as she stroked in unison with Tom. Her body streamed with sweat. She could taste the salt on the sides of her mouth.

Meanwhile, Francisca dozed in the sun and did not offer to relieve either of the two rowers.

To block out the pain in her body Katherine ran over in her mind all those words that had been whispered in the moonlight.

Because she had given herself to him, Christopher had said she belonged to him. But she belonged to no one. And never would. Christopher had also said he loved her, that he wanted to marry her. But Katherine was no silly girl whose life could be turned upside down by words spoken by a man in the moonlight.

And yet, the more Katherine reflected on it, the more she came to believe that maybe love wasn't just a word. Maybe it was a choice. She could choose to love Christopher, or choose not to love him. The choice was hers and hers alone.

There was a great freedom in having choices.

While her body ached, her spirit soared. She felt as happy as she had ever felt in her life. She smiled at the dark-haired girl opposite her and at Tom beside her. He smiled back, stopped rowing, and pointed behind them to the west. They could just make out the coastline of America.

"I think we can safely take a rest now," he said. "We've got the wind and tide with us."

Tom stretched out his back but kept his attention focused on Francisca. "Look at her," he said to Katherine reverently. "She's so beautiful, so pure, so innocent, so simple in her chaste youth."

She's simple all right, thought Katherine while nodding in

apparent agreement. Ah Tom, she mused charitably, you could never be the man for me. Instead of courage in a woman you admire timidity, instead of audacity, docility, instead of wit, puerility. In Padua, you would have idolized Emogena.

Poor man.

"I almost forgot!" he suddenly said, disrupting her thoughts. He sat up and removed a small silk bundle from his inside pocket and handed it to her. "I've got something for you."

Katherine took it. "What is it?"

"I don't know. Your man Matto, who seems to have some sort of sixth sense, came to me last night. He asked me to give it to you when I saw you. I asked him why he didn't just give it to you himself and he said that perhaps he wouldn't see you again. That's when I got worried that news of our plan had leaked out.

"Did you tell him about it?"

"No," Katherine admitted.

"Why did he think he would not see you again if he didn't know your intentions?"

"Matto may not know my intentions but he knows me," was the only explanation she could give.

Katherine unrolled the silk. Out into her lap fell her ruby wedding necklace.

Katherine almost laughed. "Well," she said aloud to no one in particular, "he always said never to trust anyone!"

A note was wrapped around the necklace's clasp. It read:

Mistress —

Here's a parting gift for you and with it a parting warning:

Never leave your greatest treasure behind you.

— Your faithful servant,
Matto

180

Clasping the necklace in her fist, Katherine smiled. Clever as Matto was, this time he had it all wrong. She hadn't left her greatest treasure behind her, for she knew she herself was her greatest treasure.

How I've changed in a year, she thought. How everything has changed. She once had to memorize the 2000-year-old teaching of Heraclitus: "Everything flows; the world is ever in flux." But that idea, which was taught to her as yet another reason for despair, now seemed more a reason for rejoicing. Constant change was what made life an adventure. And, if she chose, every day could be the start of a new adventure, whether in Charleston or Williamsburg or New Orleans.

Or Port Royal.

ARTICLES ON BOARD THE *TAINGIRE*
BRIAN CHRISTOPHER, CAPTAIN

I. The captain and the quartermaster shall each receive two shares of a prize. The master, mate, doctor, carpenter, boatswain and gunner, one and one-quarter shares, and private gentlemen of fortune one share each.

II. Every man shall have an equal title to the fresh provisions or strong liquors at any time seized, and shall use them at pleasure unless a scarcity requires retrenchment.

III. Each man shall keep his piece, cutlass and pistols clean and fit for an engagement.

IV. Lights and candles shall be put out at eight at night.

V. If any man shall lose a limb in time of engagement, he shall have 400 pieces of eight.

VI. He that shall snap his pistol and thus set off sparks, or carry a candle without a lantern, or smoke tobacco in the hold shall suffer 40 lashes on the bare back.

VII. He that shall be found guilty of cowardice in time of engagement shall be marooned or shot.

VIII. He that shall be found guilty of gaming, or defrauding another, or striking another on board, shall be marooned or shot.

IX. He that shall be found guilty of meddling with a virtuous woman without her consent shall be shot.

X. He that shall be found guilty of carrying a woman to sea in disguise shall be shot.

"I duly swear, on this Bible, an oath of allegiance to these Articles," declared the pale young man once known as Kate the Curst, the Shrew of Padua.

Kathleen Magill

Kathleen Magill is the daughter of a Great Lakes sea captain who fell head-over-heels in love with a proper schoolteacher during the closing days of World War II. She was raised on the shores of Lake Erie, moved to California at twenty, and travels the world from her home base on a hillside overlooking the Pacific Ocean just south of San Francisco.

She has a B.A. in Philosophy, an M.A. in Far Eastern Studies, and a husband who both cooks and cleans out the kitty litter. After having several plays produced in the 1970s, she switched to copyrighting and now works as the editorial director of a leading provider of online investing services. She published her first historical novel, *Megan*, in 1983.